"Are you busy tonight?"

"Thanks," Kara said, "but really, I don't go to bars." *Not anymore.*

"So you said. But it's not like it's a rowdy honky-tonk— well, not from six to eight, anyway." Derrick smiled. "I think the wildest person in the dinner crowd is usually Lily Tate. She loves the all-you-can-eat ribs, and if the cook runs out, she gets hostile."

Kara laughed. Lily Tate was a regular customer at the bank, still feisty at seventy-eight. "Well, when you put it like that…I suppose I could come for a little while."

"Great."

Kara reached to set her glass on the table, and Derrick's gaze fell on her wedding band.

He looked as if someone had knocked the air out of him.

"That is," he added, "if your husband won't mind."

Dear Reader,

Where would I be without you? I truly appreciate each and every one of you who reads the books I write. Oftentimes the characters I create pull me into the story so deeply, I feel as though they're real people. This was definitely the case with Kara and Derrick.

As a huge fan of country music, I had a lot of fun writing a hero who plays the guitar and sings country love songs. And the fact that he's just an average guy next door made me fall in love with Derrick. (I hope you will, too!) Of course, Kara is exactly the sort of person I'd like to have for a best friend, especially since she loves horses and dogs.

Friendship is all Kara can afford when Derrick first knocks on her door. But she's soon caught up in an inner battle—trying to move forward but afraid to let go of her past. Derrick faces a similar dilemma except, like a lot of men, he hides from his problems. He soon finds out that "ignore it and it'll go away" doesn't apply here.

I hope you enjoy Derrick and Kara's story as they travel a rocky road in their search for happiness.

Please come visit my Web pages at smrw.org or superauthors.com or e-mail me at BrendaMott@hotmail.com. I love hearing from my readers.

Brenda Mott

MAN FROM MONTANA
Brenda Mott

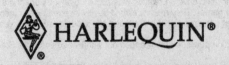

TORONTO • NEW YORK • LONDON
AMSTERDAM • PARIS • SYDNEY • HAMBURG
STOCKHOLM • ATHENS • TOKYO • MILAN • MADRID
PRAGUE • WARSAW • BUDAPEST • AUCKLAND

ISBN-13: 978-0-373-71369-1
ISBN-10: 0-373-71369-X

MAN FROM MONTANA

www.eHarlequin.com

Printed in U.S.A.

ABOUT THE AUTHOR

When Brenda isn't writing or rescuing animals—she has about thirty dogs at any given time—she enjoys curling up with a good book (naturally!), riding her horses or walking the German shepherds along the riverbank. Brenda can trace her family roots back to the Cherokees who walked the Trail of Tears, and her ranch, deep in the Tennessee woods, is located on part of what used to be the Cherokee Nation.

Books by Brenda Mott

HARLEQUIN SUPERROMANCE

Don't miss any of our special offers. Write to us at the following address for information on our newest releases.

Harlequin Reader Service
U.S.: 3010 Walden Ave., P.O. Box 1325, Buffalo, NY 14269
Canadian: P.O. Box 609, Fort Erie, Ont. L2A 5X3

This book is dedicated to my Cherokee family,
especially my dad's great-great-grandma Dancer,
who was brave enough and tough enough to walk from
the Eastern Cherokee Nation all the way to Oklahoma.
Nv-wa-do-hi-ya-dv, e-ni-si. Peace, Grandmother.
We got ten acres back.

*Phonetic pronunciation of Cherokee words translated from the
Cherokee Syllabary.*

PROLOGUE

Summer 1993

DERRICK WAS IN THE MOOD TO PLAY. He pulled his '68 Gran Torino to a halt at the only stoplight in town. Beside him, Nick Taylor smirked and revved the engine of his Chevelle.

"Hey, loser!" Nick challenged through the car's open window. "Let's see what you've got."

From the Chevelle's passenger seat, Jason Fremont sneered at him. "Your Torino sucks, Mertz, you drop-out hick!"

Nick and Jason had graduated last year and gone on to college, while he'd stayed right here in Sage Bend, Montana. Being the father of a two-year-old and holding down a full-time job didn't leave much time for anything else.

But tonight Derrick felt like the boy he used to be—the boy he sometimes wished he still was. Just a guy out celebrating his nineteenth birthday. Even if Shelly had tried to ruin it by dropping Connor off on his doorstep unannounced. It wasn't his weekend to take care of their son. He had planned to party with his friends, and she'd known that.

Derrick glanced into the back seat where his son sat strapped into the car seat. The little guy loved riding in the Gran Torino. They'd make their own fun.

The thud against his car door made Derrick's head snap around. He saw raw egg running down the side of the Torino and choked back a curse.

Nick and Jason howled with laughter, then took off with a squeal of tires as the light turned green.

Assholes!

Derrick put the Torino in gear. "What do you think, Connor? Want to show those jerks what for?"

"What for!" Connor replied, his dimpled cheeks reflected in the rearview mirror as he giggled.

Derrick let out the clutch, and the Gran Torino leapt forward like a big cat on the run. He'd gotten the car from his grandfather, and while it didn't look like much on the outside, he and Grandpa Mertz had made everything under the hood purr.

No way could that piece of crap Chevelle outrun him.

Rapidly shifting gears, he caught up with Nick and Jason, passing them by a half length as they sped away from town out onto the county road. Country music blared through his stereo speakers—

a song about fast cars and faster women—as Derrick watched his speedometer needle arc higher.

"Yeah!" He let out a whoop and shifted into high gear. The Torino's engine no longer purred—it roared.

Ahead, the paved road curved and narrowed down to dirt and gravel. Derrick gripped the wheel, prepared for the rough transition. Nick's Chevelle edged up beside him on the curve, crowding him as Nick tried to pass.

Derrick floored it. "Eat my dust!"

The Torino gave what he asked, leaping ahead as they came out of the curve. Derrick whooped again and glanced in his rearview mirror. Nick had dropped behind, and Derrick could see him cursing. *He wasn't so smart now.*

Derrick felt on top of the world.

Not somebody's father.

Not somebody's meal ticket.

Just a kid in a fast car.

The Charolais bull came out of nowhere, its off-white coat blending into the gray dusk. It stopped in the middle of the road and turned its head and, for a moment, Derrick looked right into the animal's eyes.

"Crap!" He jerked the wheel.

With a spray of dust and gravel, the Torino skidded onto the shoulder of the road, missing the bull by inches. The car fishtailed, and Derrick cranked the wheel in a desperate attempt to regain control. The right rear tire slid, then the front end whipped around—too far. And everything seemed to move in slow motion.

Grass and rock scraped the undercarriage. The fender struck a wooden post as the Torino rocketed across the shallow ditch, through a barbed wire fence. And rolled down the incline of the cow pasture.

Derrick couldn't get his bearings. Couldn't even tell which end was up. His head smacked the steering wheel, and his vision swam, then went black.

He awoke to silence. Disoriented.

Where was he? He blinked, then looked around as he remembered.

Nick's Chevelle was nowhere in sight. He and Jason had taken off, leaving Derrick in the middle of a pasture? Amazingly, the Torino had landed upright after rolling.

His prized possession—the car—had meant so much to him. But suddenly it meant nothing at all as the significance of the silence hit him.

"Connor?"

His heart leapt in his chest as he twisted around to look into the back.

Connor sat slumped in the twisted safety seat, a

streak of blood darkening his brown curls. Glass from the shattered windshield lay everywhere. It covered Connor's T-shirt, his jeans....

Dear God! Derrick fumbled with his seat belt. How could he have been so stupid? The buckle gave, and he clambered over the seat to reach his little boy.

"Connor? Hey, buddy." Hands shaking, he touched his son's neck and felt the faint flutter of a pulse. "Conner, wake up. Please?" He muttered a prayer.

What had he done?

He wanted to pull his son into his lap. But should he move him? Why the hell wasn't anybody coming down the road?

Frantically, he looked up. He thought he heard an approaching car.... Relief coursed through him when he saw the minivan. Derrick pushed against the door of the car, but it was caved in—jammed shut.

"Help me!" He beat it with his fist, glass shards cutting his hand. "Somebody help me—help my son!"

It took him a moment to hear the man. The Good Samaritan who'd rushed from the minivan. "Are you okay, kid?"

"Yeah—I—" He looked at Connor.

"I called 911."

Three numbers that had meant little to Derrick before now.

Three numbers that held his only hope that Connor would be all right.

He stared at Connor and prayed.

CHAPTER ONE

May 2005

KARA WOKE UP IN THE GRIP of a nightmare. Heart racing, she sat up in bed, covered in sweat. She switched on the bedside lamp as she looked at the clock. 3:00 a.m. She pushed her damp hair away from her eyes and swung her feet to the floor. Ever watchful, Lady looked up at Kara with intelligent brown eyes.

"Hey, Lady. Good girl." She stroked the collie's ruff, taking comfort in her presence. In the kitchen, she poured a glass of water and leaned against the sink while she drank. Would the nightmares never stop?

In her wildest imagination, Kara never would have seen herself as a widow at thirty. In her nightmares, she relived over and over again the knock on her door.

Every night it was the same. Evan's best friend and construction partner stood on the porch. Tom looked at her with such agony, she knew something awful had happened before he even spoke. Evan was never coming home again.

Kara forced herself to go back to bed. But she left the lamp on and tuned the radio to her favorite country station. Grateful it was Saturday, which meant the bank was closed and she didn't have to work, she slept fitfully. Sunlight woke her the second time. Streaming through the window, it gave the false impression everything was right and wonderful. Like a thousand other times in the past eight months, Kara only wanted to pull the drapes, crawl back in bed and sleep.

But she got up. She had to. Having Lady helped. The dog depended on her for everything. Kara let her out, then fed her.

She had quickly learned that exercise was one of the best ways to help lift herself out of depression. So after a shower and a light breakfast, she phoned Danita. No answer. Odd. Weather permitting, Danita rode with her almost every Saturday, even when it wasn't a Ride Away weekend. No matter; she'd stop at her house on her way to the stable. It was the warmest day this May so far, and she wasn't about to waste a moment of it.

From the spare bedroom that served as her tack room, Kara retrieved her saddle and carried it outside. She swung it into the back of the '78 Ford pickup that had been Evan's pride and joy, feeling his presence the way she always did…in everything he'd touched…. Lady tagged at her heels, waiting eagerly for Kara to open the passenger door.

"You wanna ride shotgun, hey, girl?" Kara laughed and let the collie in.

As she neared Danita's house on the corner, Kara spotted her best friend in the backyard, by the barbecue grill. She waved, but Danita didn't respond; didn't even seem to see her. Kara rounded the corner and parked in the driveway.

"Hey, you," she called as she opened the back-yard gate. "What's up?" Then Danita turned and Kara realized her eyes were red-rimmed, her expression furious.

"I'm having a ritual burning, that's what." She flung lighter fluid in a wild arc, soaking a pile of photographs and the torn remains of an album, then lit a match. Flames shot up with a whoosh.

Kara gasped. "Danita—my God, those are your wedding photos! *What* are you doing?" She laid a hand on her friend's arm.

"I'm burning every last trace of that cheating bastard out of my life, that's what," Danita said with a sniff. She tossed another stack of photos onto the fire.

"What?" She couldn't have heard right. Child-hood sweethearts, Danita and Phillip had been happily married for twenty-two years. They had a grown daughter…a beautiful home. But then, she

knew all too well that change and tragedy struck without warning. Kara tugged on Danita's arm. "Come sit down and tell me what happened."

The older woman allowed herself to be led to the patio table, where the two sat on her cushioned, wrought-iron chairs. "I caught him red-handed," Danita said without preamble. "I came home from work early last night because I wasn't feeling well. And there he was—*in our bed,* damn it! With one of his clients. Guess he took the massage therapy thing to a whole new level." Danita's dark eyes flooded and she blinked back tears, then blew her nose into a tissue. "Happy frickin' anniversary to me, huh?" She sniffed loudly. "We were supposed to go out to dinner this weekend to celebrate. How could that bastard do this?" She slammed her fist onto the table, causing the terra-cotta flowerpot to jump on its plate.

Kara tried not to let her mouth gape. "I don't even know what to say. My God! You should have called me. You could've stayed the night at my place." She shook her head. "I never, ever would've thought Phillip would cheat on you."

"That makes two of us." Danita honked into the tissue again. "What a fool I was. All those late evenings at work and the hang-up calls...I didn't think a thing about them. How stupid could I be?"

"You're not stupid." Kara squeezed Danita's hand. "You're a loving, trusting wife, and Phillip ought to be horsewhipped. As a matter of fact, I'll do it for you. Where is the slimeball?"

Danita managed a small laugh. "I kicked his ass to the curb. He's probably with the bimbo as we speak. The *puta!*"

Kara opened her mouth to add a snappy comment, but froze. "Oh, hell! Your porch—it's on fire!"

"What?" Danita spun in her chair, then stood so fast it tipped over. "Oh my God!"

The barbecue grill stood a short distance from the old-fashioned, shingle-roofed porch, and the breeze had caught the flames, sending them skyward. From there, they must've enveloped a hanging wicker flower basket suspended from the porch beam before the beam itself caught fire.

Kara dived for the water faucet, turning the handle on full blast as Danita pointed the hose at the porch. But the charcoal fluid must've splashed the porch. The accelerant gave the fire enough of a boost to quickly climb the beam toward the shingles. And like that, the roof was on fire.

"Call 911!" Danita shouted.

Kara was already scrambling for the cell phone in her purse.

The volunteer fire department arrived within minutes. Siren blaring, the old-but-still-reliable truck ground to a halt at the curb. Kara stood out of the way with Danita, and watched the men battle the flames. Local police officers arrived to help keep the crowding neighbors back. And because there generally wasn't a lot of excitement in Sage Bend, population eight hundred seventy-five, it took five officers arriving in three police cars to do the job.

The fire chief, Shawn Rutherford, came over to speak with Danita and Kara, and take down a report of what had happened. Tall, with thick hair that was more black than silver, Shawn had the sexiest dark eyes Kara had ever seen. And those eyes seemed fastened on Danita.

When he walked away, Kara nudged Danita in the ribs. "Hey, I think he likes you." She grinned, wanting to take her friend's mind off her troubles. "He couldn't take his eyes off you."

"Don't be ridiculous," Danita scoffed. "He was only looking at me because we were talking."

"Mmm-hmm. He talked to me, too, but he didn't look at me like that."

"After what my swine of a husband did, a man is the last person I want near me—ever again." Danita clutched her hair with both hands and stared at the smoldering porch roof. "Argh! Thank you, Phillip, for turning me into an arsonist!"

Kara draped her arm around her friend's shoulders. "When Phillip sees you out on the town with a hot fireman on your arm, he'll wish he'd never cheated on you."

Danita snorted. "Sorry to disappoint you, girl-friend, but Chief Rutherford stands a better chance of putting out the fires of Hades than he does of getting me out on a date." She crossed her arms. "And may Phillip rot in hell while he tries."

THAT NIGHT, Kara lay against her pillows on the bed she'd shared with Evan, and stared at his picture. Here she was, out of her mind missing her husband, while Danita was cursing hers and wishing him dead. Life sure didn't seem fair.

Oh, Evan, how can you be gone? Please, God, let me wake up tomorrow morning and find it's all been a bad dream. She lifted the five-by-seven photograph from the nightstand and clutched it to her breast, letting the tears come. She'd loved Evan since junior high, and they'd had a good life—a great life—together.

Kara closed her eyes, and images of Evan's funeral came back as clearly as if it had been yesterday. Snow falling from a lifeless, gray sky…Evan's friends acting as pallbearers. Big, macho construction workers who'd broken down and wept like babies over their friend's coffin. And Evan's mother, Liz—a widow herself… The poor woman needed tranquilizers.

Why? The question was one Kara still had no answer to.

She visited Evan's grave every week, often with Liz. But somehow she felt foolish, sitting beside a cold, marble stone. Evan wasn't there. His spirit was here, with her—always.

But tonight the bedroom felt empty.

The knock on her front door startled her. Lady barked and raced for the living room. Quickly, Kara dried her eyes, and placed Evan's picture back on the nightstand. Who would be knocking at this hour? It was nearly nine-thirty. She hurried after the collie.

Kara peered through one of the glass rectangles on either side of the door. A man stood on her porch.

Leaving the safety chain in place, she flicked on the porch light and opened the door a few inches. Her gaze immediately met his. He was good-looking beyond reason, his sandy-brown hair just long enough to touch the collar of the denim jacket he wore over a fancy western shirt. Tall, he looked down at her.

"Hi." He smiled. "I'm sorry to bother you at this hour, but I saw your lights on and thought you might not be asleep."

Kara stared at him through the crack. "Can I help you with something?" she asked.

"Actually, yes. I'm Derrick Mertz. I live over there." He gestured toward the mint-green house diagonally across the street from her. "And I'm afraid my kitten is stuck in the tree in your backyard."

Didn't serial killers often use the ruse of a missing pet to lure their victims? Later, the body turns up in the woods, bones scattered by wild animals. The news reporters always marveled that a crime like that could happen in such a quiet, close-knit community.

"I wasn't aware the house had sold," Kara said, preparing to slam the door in his face. She couldn't remember if the realtor's sign had still been there when she'd driven past today.

His smile disarmed her. "Actually, I haven't got much of my stuff moved in yet. But I brought my cat over, and he got out the back door. He's going to make me late getting to work if I don't catch him quick. Mind if I go into your yard?"

What could she say? "I guess that would be fine. I mean, sure. The gate's on the other side of the house."

"Thanks." He turned and hurried down the steps.

Kara closed and locked the door, including the dead bolt. "Some watchdog you are," she said to Lady as the collie merely wagged her tail. "You could've at least growled at him."

Kara hurried to the kitchen and peeked through the curtains at the well-lit yard, spotting a dark orange, half-grown kitten in the branches of her cottonwood tree.

Kara pulled on her Tony Lamas and stepped outside, Lady at her heels. Derrick stood at the base of the tree, speaking in a gentle, coaxing tone. His voice gave Kara goose bumps, but she told herself it was only the chilly night air.

"He's cute," she said, nearing the tree. "Hey, kitty."

The cat meowed, the bell on his collar jingling as he stretched hesitantly toward the next lower branch.

"Come on, Taz," Derrick coaxed. "I've got to go back to work, buddy."

"Where do you work?" Kara asked, folding her arms against her chest for warmth. She should've grabbed a jacket.

"The Silver Spur," he said. "I'm a bartender and aspiring country singer."

Kara couldn't help but smile. "You play in the band?"

"Every other Saturday, and most Fridays. Tonight I'm just bartending. I'm on my dinner break. Wasn't really hungry, so I thought I'd run out here and finish unloading a few things…check on Taz." He turned back to the kitten. At about six foot one or so, Derrick was able to stretch his long arms up and finally grab the wayward Taz.

The tabby yowled and dug its claws into the front of Derrick's shirt, hissing and spitting as it caught sight of Lady. "Ouch, you little varmint." Derrick cradled Taz against his chest. "Thanks again." He held out his free hand. "I didn't catch your name."

Hesitantly, she took it. "Kara Tillman." His hand was strong, his fingers callused from playing the guitar.

"Nice to meet you, Kara." He eyed her boots and jeans. "A cowgirl, huh?"

"Well, a wanna-be anyway." She smiled again. "I've got a horse, though."

"Do you like country music?"

"Sure."

"Why don't you come on down to the Silver Spur? The band that's playing tonight is good." He winked. "Of course, next weekend when Wild Country is playing, the music will be even better."

Suddenly she felt sick to her stomach. How many nights had she spent dancing with Evan to the beat of some country tune? "Thanks, but I'm not really into the whole bar scene."

"Well, if you change your mind, the invitation's always open." He patted Lady's head, then scrambled to clutch the kitten once more as it nearly got away from him. "Nice meeting you, Kara. Take it easy."

"You, too."

He disappeared into the shadows on the far side of the house, and Kara heard the gate swing open, then click shut as he latched it.

She stood for a moment, listening to the wind stir through the trees. Then, rubbing her hands up and down her arms, Kara called Lady back into the house and closed the door.

CHAPTER TWO

Late May

DERRICK OPENED the curtains near the foot of Connor's bed to let the sunlight stream in. Today was the last day of school, and Connor would be home at Shelly's in less than an hour, ready for Derrick to pick him up. He wanted everything perfect for his son at their new house.

He raised the window, letting the fresh air blow through the long-closed bedroom. Taz promptly jumped up on the windowsill and stared through the screen at the birds on the lawn, flicking the end of his orange tail.

Derrick laughed. "Bird buffet, huh, Taz?" He scratched the kitten's ears, enjoying the view himself. An apple tree grew near the window, its branches loaded with pinkish-white flowers. Their fragrance drifted in, mingling with the scent of damp soil and dust. A comforting, earthy smell. *Home.* So much better than that damned cramped apartment, where the neighbors constantly complained about his guitar playing.

Whistling, Derrick snapped open a fitted sheet he'd taken from the dryer a moment ago, and set about making up Connor's twin bed. He'd wanted to buy something better, a double bed for sure, but money was tight. Connor's medical bills and physical therapy had been an ongoing expense, and a not-so-famous country singer/bartender didn't make the sort of money Toby Keith and Brad Paisley likely brought home.

With the bedsheets and a dark blue comforter in place, Derrick surveyed the room. He hadn't hung a lot of stuff on the walls—he wanted Connor to make the place his own. Just a couple of things he thought the boy might like, including an autographed poster of Shania Twain one of the guys in his band had gotten for Connor at a recent concert.

The room looked kind of plain, with only the twin bed, a secondhand chest of drawers and a computer stand for Connor's laptop in the corner. Derrick had paid for Internet service, even though he didn't have any use for it himself, didn't even own a computer. But he couldn't expect the kid to spend every waking minute with him, even though Derrick would've preferred it that way.

His time with his son was precious. The days between his weekend visits seemed an eternity, while the two or three days he had with Connor sped by. Even the longer summer visitations seemed far too short. But it beat the hell out of the supervised, three-hour visits he'd once had.

Satisfied the room was as good as it was going to get, Derrick got the keys to his truck, and his guitar and headed out the door. He couldn't wait to pick Connor up. Their every-other-Friday-night ritual of stopping by the local burger joint was something he looked forward to. And tonight, he had band practice. Since a love for country music and double cheeseburgers seemed to be two of the few things he and his son shared these days, Derrick intended to make the most of it.

As he neared his pickup, he spotted Kara, struggling out her front door with an armload of tack, including a heavy-looking western saddle and thick saddle pad. The pretty strawberry-blonde had bumped the screen open with one hip, and now attempted to pull the door shut behind her, her collie at her heels.

Derrick was across the street in a few loping strides.

"Hang on. Let me help you."

She glanced over her shoulder at him and grimaced. "Thanks, but I've got it. I'm used to doing this." But she let him hold the screen and finish closing the door for her. "Make sure it's locked, please." She watched as he jiggled the knob. "Thanks."

"Going riding?" Then he laughed, bending to pat the dog. "Well, I guess that's obvious. Taking advantage of the longer daylight hours, huh?"

Her freckled nose crinkled as she smiled. "Yep. I go every chance I get."

"Really? Maybe I ought to get myself a horse."

Immediately, Kara stopped smiling.

"I hate to be rude, but I'm in a hurry." She swung the saddle and blanket into the back of her pickup—a sharp-looking, black Ford. "I'm meeting some friends."

"Yeah. Sure." *She didn't have to knock him over the head with a riding crop.* He leaned against the truck bed, and glanced at the bridle and grooming tools she'd already loaded. "Don't they have a tack room at your stable?"

"Yes. But things tend to grow legs and wander off. Or so I've heard. I prefer keeping my stuff at home."

"Ah. I can understand that."

"You'd better get your guitar," she said, softening her words with a half smile. "Before it grows legs."

He'd forgotten he'd set it down in the middle of his driveway. "Yeah. I've got practice with the guys tonight. We're playing tomorrow." He hesitated. She hadn't taken him up on his invite last weekend…should he ask her again?

"Have fun." She opened the truck door, and the collie jumped in.

"You, too."

He watched Kara drive away.

Going riding?

Hell.

Maybe instead of band practice, he ought to relearn how to ask a woman out.

KARA PULLED AWAY from the curb, her eyes drawn to Derrick Mertz in the rearview mirror. He waved, and she immediately averted her gaze, embarrassed he'd caught her looking. Twice. What the hell was wrong with her? *I'm sorry, Evan.*

She leaned back in her seat, steering the Ford with one hand, resting her other wrist lightly on top of the wheel.

Evan had fixed up the truck himself, painting it gloss black, redoing the engine…the interior. He'd washed and waxed the Ford regularly, and she'd loved helping him.

They'd done everything together. On the weekends, they often went cruising, Kara snuggled next to Evan, his arm around her as though they were still dating. Six years of marriage had changed nothing in terms of romance. For them, the honeymoon hadn't ended once they'd fallen into the everyday aspects of married life, the way it had for many of their friends.

Friends who'd drifted away after Evan's death. A single woman—a widow—did not fit neatly into the group. Thank God for Danita, and even Liz, who had lost a husband and a son, and depended heavily on her. Liz had always been like a second mother to Kara. She and Evan had even moved to Sage Bend to be near her when Evan's dad died.

But at times she wished Liz would lend her a shoulder for a change. With Kara's own parents living back in Colorado, she often felt homesick. She'd lost so much when she'd lost Evan.

And now, here she was ogling a good-looking cowboy singer in the rearview mirror of her husband's pickup.

Guilt-ridden, Kara slipped on her sunglasses to shield her eyes from the glare of the late afternoon sun, then placed both hands firmly on the steering wheel. She'd ride her troubles away, just like she always did.

At the stable, Kara led Indio to a hitching post and began to brush her, while Lady nosed around the area. Her informal riding group had decided to take an early evening trail ride, since rain was predicted for Saturday. Within minutes, Danita arrived and got busy saddling her mount, soon followed by Beth Murphy, another of the Ride Away members.

"Hi," Kara greeted her.

"Hey," Beth said, blowing a strand of her short

blond hair out of her eyes and giving Lady a pat. Beth was forty-three, but she looked much younger. "How was work today?"

"Busy. Fridays are always crazy. Thank God I didn't have to stay to work the drive-up window." She saddled her Appaloosa, waving to Hannah Williamson, the fourth—and final—Ride Awayer, as she pulled up, horse trailer in tow. The local large animal vet, Hannah took care of the horses at the boarding stable, and owned a twenty-five-acre ranch not far from there.

While Beth went into the barn to get her horse and Hannah unloaded Ricochet, Kara seized the opportunity to question Danita. "Are you doing okay, hon?" She'd been worried about her friend, keeping tabs on her all week by phone.

"I'm hanging in." Danita shrugged. "Trying to focus on repainting the house. I might as well make a few changes, now that Phillip has officially moved out. He picked up the last of his stuff yesterday." She set her jaw. "The rat. He's already got a new place with a swimming pool. I hope he gets skin cancer."

Kara couldn't help but chuckle. "I didn't know rats liked water."

"Sure they do. That's why the ones in New York hang out in the sewers." Danita laughed, too. "Speaking of men, I passed by your house on my way home from the store before I came out here, and I saw Derrick Mertz in your yard."

"You know him?"

"Sort of. Phillip and I used to go to the Silver Spur once in a while."

"I didn't know that." Personally, she'd never paid much attention to the band when she'd gone with Evan. She'd only had eyes for her husband.

"So what was he doing at your place?" Danita arched an eyebrow.

Kara squirmed. "He's my new neighbor. He helped me load my tack into the truck."

"Uh-huh." Danita licked her lips and smiled. "I waved at you as I passed, but you drove right by me. I think you were too busy looking in your rearview mirror to notice."

"I shouldn't have done that."

"Done what?"

"Lusted after another man."

"*Mi hija.*" Danita laid a soothing hand on her arm. "Evan's gone. You can only be alone for so long."

Kara knew her friend meant well, but didn't want to ever replace Evan in her heart. "I miss him so much." She bit her lip.

"Of course you do. But you're young, and so pretty." Danita gave her a hug. "You'll find happiness again. Unlike me, a middle-aged janitor with wrinkles and gray hair."

"I heard that," Beth said, as she led her chestnut

mare, Sundance, toward the hitching rail. She elbowed Danita in the ribs. "I'm older than you, and you do *not* have gray hair."

"Thanks to my hairdresser." Danita grimaced. "Too bad he's gay. He's really good-looking."

Hannah walked over, leading her saddled gelding. "That's always the way it goes," she said. "But you stop putting yourself down." She frowned at Danita, tossing her brown ponytail over one shoulder. "You run your own cleaning business, woman. And you're smart, beautiful and in the prime of your life. To hell with Phillip."

"That's right," Beth said. "As soon as the men in this town find out you're single, they'll be flocking around like ants at a picnic." She tightened her cinch. "And you might as well start tonight. Hannah and I are going to the Silver Spur. Come with us. You, too, Kara."

Kara shook her head, gathering Indio's reins. "I'm not much for the bar scene."

"All right, I'll go," Danita said. "But I'm not cruising for guys. I need another man like I need another twenty pounds of fat on my ass."

Kara laughed.

Horses tacked up, the four women set off along the bridle path. Hannah moved Ricochet up beside Indio, as Danita and Beth rode ahead. "I wish you'd change your mind about coming tonight."

Kara wished her friends would quit pressuring her. "I don't think so."

Hannah's hazel eyes held compassion. "I know you're still grieving, and that you need time. But be careful not to let it consume you, either. Life's too short, kiddo."

"Tell me about it," Kara snapped. She couldn't help but resent Hannah's comment. What did she know about losing a husband? Twenty-nine—the only single woman in the group—Hannah had her whole life ahead of her. Evan hadn't even been around to celebrate Kara's thirtieth birthday. "My time with Evan flew by. Like that." She snapped her fingers.

"I'm sorry," Hannah said. Her gaze held Kara's, full of such sympathy, Kara felt like a bitch.

"It's okay." She fought the familiar, choking ache in the back of her throat. Tears stung her eyes, but she blinked them back.

Hannah's words had hit home.

Kara's biggest fear was being exactly like her mother-in-law…grieving forever.

Never getting over the loss of the man she'd loved with all her heart and soul.

SATURDAY BROUGHT some cloud cover, but the rain held off, the temperature hovering in the mid-fifties. Kara opted to do some yard work midmorning, determined to get the soil along the front wall of her house turned, so she could plant some bachelor buttons and Shasta daisies. As she went to work with a shovel, the sound of guitar music floated her way. Pausing, she listened, then smiled. Someone was singing a popular country tune. But it didn't sound like Derrick. Maybe one of his band?

Puzzled, Kara leaned the shovel against the wall. The voice sounded young, more like a kid's. She started across the lawn, then hesitated. What was she doing? She should mind her own business and tend to her flower bed. Kara picked up the shovel again and turned over another section of dirt.

But the guitar music lifted her spirits—a rare thing these days. She simply couldn't resist seeing who the player was.

A few minutes later, Kara paused on Derrick's front walkway. Near the open door, a porch swing and two chairs stood empty, the orange tabby kitten dozing beneath one of them. The wraparound porch hid the guitar player from view, the music coming from the side of the house.

What the heck. She was already here.

Kara climbed the steps and called out as she rounded the corner of the porch. "Hello?"

For a moment, the boy didn't see or hear her. And Kara didn't realize he was sitting in a wheelchair. Her eyes darted to the chair a split second later, then back up just as the kid's gaze met hers. He blushed, breaking off midtune, his hand resting across the top of the guitar, a pick in his fingers. "Can I help you with something?"

She felt awkward. "I'm sorry. I didn't mean to intrude." Kara gestured over her shoulder. "I live across the street. I heard the guitar...."

"Sorry about that." The boy's face reddened deeper beneath his light-brown hair. "Dad thought guitar music wouldn't bother the neighbors anymore, since he moved out of his apartment."

Dad.

Wow. She'd assumed Derrick was a single man, living alone. Somehow she hadn't expected a guitar-picking, bartending cowboy to have a half-grown son.

"You weren't bothering me at all," Kara hastened to explain, as the boy fumbled to put the instrument back in its case. "I came over because I liked what I heard. I wanted to see who was playing."

He paused, looking skeptically at her. "Really?"

"You bet. I'm a big country music fan." She held out her hand. "I'm Kara Tillman."

He shook hands briefly. "Connor."

"Well, Connor, I can see you're following in your dad's footsteps. He must be proud."

"Don't tell him."

The boy's hasty comment took her by surprise. "Excuse me?"

"Don't tell my dad I was playing his guitar. Please."

She didn't know what to say. "All right." Was Derrick touchy about his guitar? To the point that he wouldn't let his own son play it?

Before she could say anything else, they heard the sound of a car pulling into the driveway.

"Damn!" Connor hastened to wheel his chair through the sliding doors off the side porch, guitar case in his lap. He bumped the case into the door-jamb, and cursed again.

Kara wasn't sure why she moved to help him, but she did. "Here." She didn't even know the boy, but the thought of Derrick getting angry at him for something that seemed harmless to her, somehow made her want to protect Connor. She righted the case and, reaching over his shoulders, balanced it on his lap as he wheeled into the house. Her adrenaline surged, and she felt silly.

Once Connor was safely inside, Kara hurried around to the front porch again. She spotted Derrick gathering a double handful of plastic grocery sacks from the camper shell on his pickup.

"Hi," she called.

He looked up, surprised. "Hi, yourself." He frowned curiously as he walked toward her. "So, what's up?"

Suddenly Kara realized that in helping Connor hide his secret, she no longer had an excuse to be at Derrick's house. She fumbled for an answer. "Oh—

nothing really. I, uh—" Crud! "—was doing a little yard work, and I made too much lemonade, and I wondered if you'd like some." She smiled, hoping her expression didn't look as lame as her excuse felt. "But Connor said you weren't here."

"Oh, you met him then?" He smiled, not at all like the sort of dad who would mind his son playing his guitar.

"Yes. He's a nice kid."

They reached the sliding doors that opened off the kitchen, just as Connor came back outside. He held a glass of water between his knees, and Kara nearly laughed out loud. They'd thought of similar excuses for their odd behavior.

Derrick didn't seem to notice. "Hey, buddy, you want to take these and I'll go back for the rest?" He handed the grocery bags off to the boy.

"Yeah, sure." Connor set his water glass on a small, round table near the door, then took the bags, set them in his lap and wheeled back inside.

"Need another hand?" Kara asked.

"If you want. One more trip ought to do it."

Kara lifted a couple of the bags from the truck. Inside the kitchen, she looked around, appreciating the fact that it was fairly neat. Only a glass and a sandwich plate sat in the sink. A dish drainer on the countertop held a few items, things that looked as though they might not fit in the dishwasher. The entire room was sparsely furnished and decorated, but somehow homey, the walls painted a cheerful yellow. But no woman's touch, and Kara wondered where Connor's mother was.

"So, where's the lemonade?" Derrick asked.

"What?"

"The lemonade you made too much of?" The corner of his mouth quirked. "Isn't that what Connor had in his glass?" He hooked a thumb over his shoulder toward the table on the porch.

"No, that's just water," Connor said. He looked at her, puzzled.

Crap! "I guess you got thirsty, what with all our yakking." Kara smiled, then looked at Derrick. "The lemonade's at my place. I didn't want to bring it over until I was sure you wanted it, but I'll go get it now." *Stop babbling.* "See you in a bit." She headed for the door.

Back across the street, she hurried to her cupboard, glad she'd bought a can of powdered, pink-lemonade mix at the store last week. She felt like an idiot. Derrick probably thought she'd made up some lame story so she could barge over to his house. With his good looks, combined with that sexy cowboy image and the fact that he sang and played the guitar, he probably had women lining up on his doorstep. Probably not bearing pink lemonade, but she could only imagine what the others brought him.

She'd make sure Derrick knew she wasn't that type.

Plastic pitcher in hand, Kara headed back across the street. She'd drop the lemonade off and leave.

This time it was Derrick who had the guitar out when she reached the porch. He sat in a chair near the table. In his wheelchair, Connor munched on a stick of beef jerky. Derrick laid the guitar down and reached for one of three plastic tumblers he'd set out.

"It's mighty nice of you to bring the lemonade. Have a seat." He gestured to an empty chair, then poured her some of the drink before she could refuse.

"No problem. Like I said, I made too much."

"Well, it was still nice." He took a sip, his long, strong fingers curled around the tumbler. Connor had poured himself some lemonade, and he took a big gulp, not saying anything. But he cast her a grateful look.

They sat in silence for a while. Kara began to feel awkward. She should leave.

"Are you busy tonight?" Derrick asked.

Kara tensed. "I'm not sure what I'm doing yet."

"It's family night at the Silver Spur. They have it the first and last Saturday of every month. They open up the dining area, and serve soft drinks and appetizers from six until eight, or dinner if you want it. That way the kids can listen to the band for a while—maybe dance a little—before things get kicking in the bar."

During the week, the Spur doubled as the local steakhouse. After dinner hours, a sliding partition closed the dining room off from the bar. She and Evan had eaten there a few times.

"Why don't you come?" Derrick suggested. "You can sit with Connor so he won't feel bored and alone."

"I'm not a baby, Dad," Connor said. "I don't care if I sit by myself."

Didn't the boy have friends from school?

"Thanks," Kara said, "but really, I don't usually go to bars." *Not anymore.*

"So you said." He nodded. "But it's not like it's a rowdy honky-tonk—well, not from six to eight anyway." He smiled. "I think the wildest person in the dinner crowd is usually Lily Tate. She loves the all-you-can-eat ribs, and if the cook runs out, she gets hostile."

Kara laughed. Lily Tate was a regular customer at the bank, still feisty at seventy-eight. "Well, when you put it that way. I suppose I could come for a little while."

"Great."

Kara reached to set her lemonade glass on the table and, as she did, Derrick's gaze fell on her wedding band.

He looked like someone had knocked the air out of him.

"That is," he added, "if your husband won't mind."

CHAPTER THREE

KARA DIDN'T ANSWER for a long, drawn-out minute. Derrick waited. How could he have missed the ring on her left hand? Maybe because it was just a simple, white-gold band.

"My husband was killed eight months ago."

Her quiet answer almost didn't register. *Shit.* "Kara, I'm sorry." Derrick wished he could wind the clock back five minutes and start over. Out of the corner of his eye, he saw the look Connor gave him and felt even worse. "I shouldn't have jumped to conclusions. It's just that—"

She held up her hand. "Don't worry about it. I can imagine you get all sorts of women falling all over you at the bar."

That made him sound like a womanizer. "Well, not exactly, but I have had married women ask me out before."

"I wasn't the one doing the asking."

She bit her lip, and he could see she was trying not to cry. He felt like the dirt under a worm's belly.

"Kara—"

"Derrick, it's okay." She stood. "I'd better get back to my flower bed."

"Then you'll still come?"

She nodded. "Connor, it was real nice meeting you. I'll see you later."

"Yeah, sure."

Derrick watched her walk away, still feeling awful.

"Way to go, Dad."

"Hey, how did I know?"

Connor merely shrugged.

Derrick strummed his guitar, playing but not singing. The image of Kara's sad expression kept running through his mind. He'd be sure to do his best to make her smile tonight. Music was the best way he knew to ease sorrow.

"Connor, are you sure you don't have any friends you want to invite to the Spur tonight?" It worried him that his son was a loner, the majority of his friends e-pals.

"I'm sure."

"What about Kevin?" Connor's classmate was the only kid he ever hung out with. Most of the others couldn't see past Connor's wheelchair.

"He's got soccer practice today. His mom takes the team out for pizza afterward, and then he'll probably spend the night at John Brody's house."

"Oh." It hurt Derrick more than words could say

that his son wasn't able to take part in sports. It was yet another thing he'd taken from the boy.

"I'm gonna go check my e-mail," Connor said.

"All right." Derrick watched him wheel away, wishing there was something he could do for him. He'd give anything if Connor could join his school-mates on the soccer team, or the rodeo team next year, or whatever else he cared to do.

He just wanted his son to be happy.

The phone rang, and Derrick grabbed it off the hook. "Hello?"

There was no answer, and he nearly hung up, thinking it was a computerized telemarketer.

"Hello, son. How are you?"

"Mom?" His heart raced. His mother never called, even waited to talk to Connor when he was at Shelly's. "What's the matter?"

"Nothing. I—" Her voice cracked and she began to cry.

"What is it? Did something happen to Dad?" He hadn't spoken two words to his father since the accident, and not much more than that to his mom. Connor spent time with them, but Derrick had lost contact after they'd moved to Miles City—more than two hundred miles away.

"Mom?"

"No, it's not your father. I, uh, just got out of the hospital a few days ago. I had to have some surgery."

Fear gripped him. "For what?"

"The doctor found tumors on my ovaries. And boy, did that scare the hell out of me." She sniffed. "You don't know how many times I've started to pick up the phone to call you."

"Why didn't you?" But he knew why.

"Well, you know how your father is."

"So, why are you calling now? You're all right, aren't you?"

"I'm fine. I had to have a hysterectomy, but there's no sign of cancer, thank God."

Derrick let out the breath he didn't know he'd been holding. "I'm glad to hear that."

"Anyway, all this got me thinking about how life really is too short. Son, I want to make things right between us. I'm so sorry for the way I've treated you. I—"

"Carolyn!" In the background, Derrick heard his father's booming voice. "What the hell do you think you're doing?"

Her reply was muffled.

"She's hanging up now, Derrick—" Vernon spoke into the phone, his voice as cold as steel "—and don't try calling her back. She's out of her mind on painkillers. That's all."

The line went dead. Derrick stared at the phone for a long moment before hanging it up.

He'd nearly killed their only grandchild.

His dad would never forgive him.

THE SILVER SPUR looked more like a barn than a bar, painted a faded gray-brown to give it a weathered appearance. Three miles outside of town, the honky-tonk stood in the middle of a field near the intersection of two dirt roads.

Kara had decided to drive to the Spur early, to avoid arriving in the midst of a huge crowd. She needed to ease her way into this evening. She'd nurse a beer while she waited for Connor and Derrick, and hopefully get a grip on her nerves. The only reason she'd accepted Derrick's invitation was because she'd decided Hannah was right. She needed to get out and do something for herself, before her grief drowned her.

And she planned to make it clear to Derrick that she hadn't come here tonight for him. But when Kara pulled into the parking lot, Derrick's truck was already there. Parked beside a van and another pickup, Derrick was busy unloading band equipment along with three other guys. Connor hovered nearby, watching. He raised his hand in greeting, and Kara took a step backward. Of course Wild Country would arrive early to set up before the crowd.

Derrick spotted her, too, and she let out a groan. He probably thought she'd arrived early because she couldn't wait. This, on top of the lemonade fiasco, was too much.

Not knowing what else to do, Kara got out of the Ford and walked over to say hi.

"You're here early," Derrick said. He looked way too fine in his black cowboy hat, teal-blue western shirt and tight jeans.

"Yep. I plan to get a good table."

"Smart. Just let me haul some of this stuff in and I'll be right with you."

"No worries. Connor can walk me in." She turned and smiled at the boy, who was dressed in boots, faded jeans and a T-shirt with the picture of country singer Gretchen Wilson. "Is that all right with you, Connor?"

He shrugged. "Sure." Deftly, he maneuvered his wheelchair across the dirt-and-gravel parking lot.

Kara walked beside him, wondering not for the first time what had caused the boy to be confined to the chair. Kara couldn't imagine being in his situation.

"So, would you like to sit with me?" she asked. "It's been a while since I've been here, and I hate sitting alone."

"Sure."

Drawing conversation out of the kid was like trying to coax a mule along with a piece of twine.

Farther on, the parking lot's hard-packed surface became rutted, making the going somewhat difficult for Connor. He seemed to have a fair amount of upper body strength, his arms thin yet wiry. But it couldn't be easy to wheel across this. Should she offer to help? Kara fought the urge to take hold of the wheelchair's handles, sensing her gesture would not be welcomed.

At that moment, she heard the sound of teenaged laughter. She looked up to see a group of three boys and two girls, somewhere close to Connor's age, walking through the nearby field. They stared at Connor as they passed. One of the boys said something, and the others laughed.

Connor shot the boy a look that would've stripped varnish off furniture. Kara's heart ached for him. She remembered adolescence all too well, getting teased for being too skinny and wearing braces.

Only Evan had seen her in a different light.

Lost in thought, Kara barely noticed the huge pothole, stepping around it at the last minute. And Connor, wheeling the chair too hard in his anger, wasn't really watching where he was going. Kara gasped as the wheel on one side of his chair dropped into the hole.

Before she could call out a warning, the boy tilted at a precarious angle, then tipped sideways. He thrust out his right arm and awkwardly caught himself, barely managing to keep the wheelchair from tipping completely over. But he couldn't hold that position long and, wiry or not, he wasn't strong enough to right himself.

Kara moved to help, but Derrick beat her to it.

With seemingly little effort, he righted his son's chair and steadied the boy to keep him from sliding out onto the ground. "You okay, bud?"

Connor's face turned red. "I'm fine! Jeez!" The kids were still staring and snickering, and his face turned an even deeper shade. "What are you looking at?"

"Not much, you little queer," the tallest boy sneered.

"Screw off, asshole!"

"Connor!" Derrick frowned. "Watch your language."

But the anger on his face matched Kara's own. She wanted to race over and give them a piece of her mind—and a swift kick to their bratty butts.

It didn't help that Derrick's reprimand embarrassed Connor even more. He thrust his palms against the wheels of his chair, sending it flying across the parking lot in a way Kara was afraid would cause him to crash again.

Calling out a final round of taunts, the teens hurried away across the field, then turned down the dirt road.

Kara rushed to catch up with Connor, Derrick on her heels.

"Looks like you could use some peroxide," she said. Connor's palm was skinned, and his elbow scraped.

"I said I'm fine. You guys don't need to make such a big deal out of it."

Derrick grunted. "Yeah, well, if it's not a big deal, then pour some peroxide on your road rash." He rested one hand on his hip. "I'll bet Tina has some in her first-aid kit in the back. Why don't you go on in and ask her?" He looked at Kara. "Tina owns the Spur."

"Oh—yes, I think I met her once."

He raised his eyebrows. "Really? I thought you didn't hang out in bars."

"I don't." She shrugged. "But Evan and I used to come here to dance once in a while."

Derrick nodded. "Guess I'd better haul in my stuff. See you later." He clamped his hand on Connor's shoulder, then headed back to his pickup.

"Come on," Kara said. "Let's get your elbow cleaned up."

"I can do it," Connor said. Then, as if he remembered Kara wasn't the enemy, he added, "Thanks."

"I know you can," she said. "Actually, I'm only sticking to you like glue because I'm nervous."

He looked at her, puzzled. "Why?"

She lifted a shoulder. "Like I told your dad, I haven't been here since my husband died. It's sort of hard to deal with, you know?"

The boy's expression softened. "Yeah, I guess it would be. What happened to him anyway?" He began wheeling his chair along at a more reasonable pace as they talked.

"Evan was a construction worker—he built houses. He fell off a scaffold." She took a deep breath. "The impact caused severe internal injuries. Nothing could be done to save him."

"Damn." Connor frowned. "That's gotta be tough." He was silent a moment. "I don't remember the accident that put me in this chair."

Kara watched as he navigated around another rut, was careful to keep her tone casual. "No?"

"Uh-uh. I was only two when it happened."

How hard that must've been for Derrick—and Connor's mother. Connor said he didn't remember the accident, but surely Derrick had told him the details. Kara started to press the boy for more information, then decided it wasn't her place. She wanted to ask him where his mother was, and who she was. She remembered he'd said something about his dad having moved out of *his* apartment.

Did Connor live with his mom?

"By the way, that's a sweet-looking Ford you've got."

"Thanks," Kara murmured. "It was my husband's."

"And you've got a horse?"

"Yeah, an Appaloosa."

"Cool. I like horses."

"Well, maybe you can come to my boarding stable and see her sometime."

They'd reached the side entrance and, deftly, Connor bumped his wheelchair up and over the threshold into the bar.

"I'll grab us a table," Kara said. "You can join me after you get your elbow cleaned up."

"Okay." Connor wheeled across the hardwood toward a hallway near the bar.

The room looked about the same as she remembered. The bandstand along the far wall, a scuffed but polished dance floor in a horseshoe in front of it, tables barely big enough to hold drinks—with as many chairs crammed around them as possible—scattered everywhere. Off to one side, the divider that opened up into the dining area stood open, and Kara could see bigger tables over there. She sat at one, then decided it was too far away.

Shouldering her purse, she chose a table with four chairs, close enough to get a view of the band, yet far enough from the dance floor and bar to avoid traffic.

"Hey there. What can I get you to drink, hon?"

Kara looked up at a familiar face. The waitress—a woman about her own age—smiled at her. She wore a sparkly western shirt, short, denim cutoffs and red cowboy boots. Kara couldn't remember the woman's name, but her dark red hair—sprayed and teased into a wild mane—was hard to forget.

"I'll have a Coke," Kara said. "Actually, make it two. I've got a friend joining me." Then she added as an afterthought, "And maybe an order of super nachos, if you still serve them." Connor might like some. The kid deserved a treat after what had happened outside.

"We do." The waitress scratched her order on a notepad, and Kara saw the gold heart pinned to her shirt with her name on it—Tori. "I'll be right back with your drinks."

"Thanks."

Tori brought the Cokes just as Connor got to the table. "I ordered some nachos," Kara told him, "but I wasn't sure what you'd like to drink. Is Coke okay?"

"Sure. Man, I love the super nachos." He gave her a crooked smile, dimples in his cheeks.

"So do I." Connor was a cute kid, and he looked a lot like his dad.

They sat in companionable silence, watching Derrick and his band set up. He looked their way once, and Kara quickly turned away. She was about to ask Connor what grade he'd be going into next fall, when she heard a voice she knew well.

"My, my. Look what the proverbial cat dragged in," Danita said.

Kara turned and groaned as she saw Beth and

Hannah as well. All three were dressed in their country-western finest.

"I thought you didn't do the bar scene," Beth accused her.

"And I thought you were all coming here last night," Kara replied.

"We were," Beth said, "but Hannah had an emergency call, so we postponed until tonight."

"And I'm glad we did." Danita leaned over, squeezing Kara's shoulders from behind. "We're happy you could make it, girlfriend, but isn't your date a little young?"

The boy looked embarrassed.

"Ignore her, Connor," Kara said. "She's old and senile." She laughed as Danita lightly punched her in the arm. "Danita, meet my neighbor, Connor Mertz. Connor, this is Danita—my former best friend."

"Mertz...are you Derrick's son?" She gestured toward the stage.

"Yeah." Connor glanced at his dad.

"Well, no wonder you're so handsome."

The boy took a long pull on his straw, red in the face.

Danita and Beth sat down, and Hannah pulled up an extra chair and squeezed in as well.

"Hope you don't mind sitting with girls," Hannah said.

Connor shrugged. "I guess not." He kept his eyes

down on the napkin he was shredding into ever smaller pieces.

"Just wait a few years," Beth said. "You'll be ecstatic to have so much female attention."

Connor's face clouded over. "I don't think so."

But before Kara could ponder his reaction, Hannah said, "So, Kara, what made you decide to come here after you told us no?"

Kara fingered the cuff of her lacy Western blouse and hoped she wasn't blushing as much as Connor. "I changed my mind, that's all."

"And you didn't call to tell us?" Hannah pretended to pout. "I'm crushed."

"Me, too." Beth waved over at the bar for service.

"I would have, but I thought you'd be partied out." She squirmed. For her, this was a big step, one she'd needed to take solo. "I just decided you all were right. I should get out more."

"Well, I'm glad to hear that," Danita said. "Now if we can get you drunk and dancing, my night will be complete."

"It's family night, remember?" Kara said. "And besides, I don't get drunk."

"It's family night until eight," Danita emphasized. "Cover your ears, kid. We're about to be a bad influence."

Connor rolled his eyes. "You haven't met the guys in my dad's band."

Hannah stared wistfully at the group of cowboys in tight jeans and Western hats, setting up their equipment on stage. "No, I haven't."

The women laughed.

As the barroom began to fill with patrons, Kara kept her eyes on Derrick. After introducing himself and his band, he looked her way and began to sing an upbeat song.

Beneath the table, Kara held her hands in her lap, twisting her wedding band.

Don't even think about it.

Quickly, she turned toward the generous serving of nachos Tori set down in the middle of the table. But even the melted cheese and rich sour cream couldn't distract her from the longing that overwhelmed her.

She'd lost something precious. Something she'd never have again.

The song ended, and the crowd applauded and whistled.

"Thank you," Derrick said. "This next song is one I wrote myself. It's called 'Heaven.'"

Kara watched Derrick's fingers move across the guitar strings, expecting him to croon a sentimental love song. Instead, he sang something far different.

"As we flew out of Denver
My little boy said to me,

'Daddy, how high up is heaven?
Are we gonna get to see
Jesus and His angels?
Will they wave at me?'
"I smiled and said 'son,
We'll just wait and see,
But I think that Heaven's higher
Than we're gonna be.'
"A few years later at the rodeo,
My son was now thirteen,
He sat down in the chute, just like his heroes
on TV…"

Kara listened closely to the words…the story of
how the father watched his son grow up riding bulls.
When the boy—now a young man—was challenged
to ride a bull no cowboy had ever been able to ride
before, she felt the father's trepidation.

And her heart broke as Derrick sang about the
young cowboy's fatal injuries, and the father's grief.

"Days later at his graveside, a memory came
to me.
Of my little boy's first airplane ride,
And what he'd asked of me.
He said, 'Daddy how high up is heaven?
Will I get to see
Jesus and His angels?

Will they wave at me?'
"And that's when I knew he'd found his way,
For when I looked on high
There was Jesus and his angels,
And my son stood by his side.
"'Daddy, how high up is hea—ven?'"

Derrick held the last note on the guitar, and the crowd erupted in whistles and cheers. In the dim light, Kara saw she wasn't the only one who had to wipe her eyes. It was easy to see where Connor had gotten his singing voice.

She glanced at the boy and wondered if he were the inspiration behind Derrick's song. Had he come close to death in whatever accident had caused his injuries?

If Derrick wanted her to know his personal business, he'd tell her. Yet she couldn't help imagining what it would be like to be held by this man. To wake up in his arms, not in an empty bed.

She told herself she ached for Evan, that it was Derrick's song that brought out her emotions. But deep down, Kara knew it wasn't just the song. It was Derrick who stirred something in her.

Something that scared her, and made her wish she hadn't come to the Silver Spur.

CONNOR MUNCHED on the nachos and the women's conversation faded to so much white noise. He'd always found it easier to talk to adults than kids, but he felt kind of stupid sitting here with four chicks. Especially since they had to be as old as his dad, or older. But then, Kara had been nice to him, and she hadn't ratted him out for playing his dad's guitar.

He watched his father up on stage, entertaining the crowd. What would it be like to be up there? To have everyone in the room focused on you? Connor had often wondered. It was exactly why he didn't want his dad to know he could play. Connor knew he'd fall short of his father's accomplishments.

After having saved his allowance for what felt like forever, he'd bought a secondhand acoustic guitar from the pawnshop, and sworn his mom to secrecy. Between video tapes, books, and trying things on his own, he'd learned to play a decent tune. He spent a lot of time picking that old guitar, and when he'd gotten the chance to play his dad's Gibson this afternoon, the temptation was too much to resist.

Playing on the side of the wraparound porch was fun. It felt almost like a stage, and yet he was blocked from anyone's view by the thick shrubbery that grew along the perimeter of the acre lot the house sat on. Plus the nearby sawmill often created a distant whine, keeping him from drawing anyone's attention. Of course, Kara had still caught him. He'd have to be more careful about playing when someone might walk up on the porch like that. He didn't want an audience, not until—and unless—he could pick the way his dad did.

Maybe one day he'd come close to being that good, if he practiced hard enough. But he could never let him know how he felt.

He sure as hell didn't want to admit how much he wished he could be like his dad. It would be so rad to play in a band and have girls falling all over him. In his daydreams, Connor was the star; the lead singer. Women went wild over him. They swooned, and threw their underwear at the stage, the way he'd heard women often did when things got rowdy at a concert.

But that's all his thoughts were. Stupid dreams.

Everyone knew women didn't fall for some guy in a wheelchair.

And if dumb-ass Bart Denson and his loser friends knew he fancied himself a guitar player—a country one at that—he'd never live it down.

Connor recalled how the girls who'd been with ol' Fart-Bart earlier had stared at him when he'd tipped his chair. *God,* he'd wanted to die right then and there, humiliated. And that made him furious. It seemed to be the only way girls ever looked at him— with pity or morbid curiosity.

Nope. He'd never be like his dad.

And he'd be damned if he'd ever let anyone know how much that bothered him.

CHAPTER FOUR

DERRICK FINISHED his first set and announced a break to the audience. He shrugged out of his guitar strap, and carefully leaned the Gibson on a stand. He hadn't missed the way Kara had focused on him as he sang.

With a cloth, he wiped the sweat from his forehead. Two women were sitting at the table with her and Connor. The blonde looked familiar, and he'd possibly seen the dark-haired one here once or twice as well. Hannah Williamson had arrived earlier but must've left already.

Feeling a natural high that stemmed from his music, Derrick headed their way, bottled water in hand. The atmosphere of the Silver Spur surrounded him like an old friend.

"Still here, I see." He grinned and pulled out a chair between Kara and Connor.

"Of course," she said. "Your band's great."

"So we didn't run you off, then?"

"Are you kidding?" said the blond woman. "You guys ought to be in Nashville."

Derrick laughed. "I don't know about that." He took a swig of water just as Dr. Williamson rejoined the group, coming from the direction of the ladies room. She was his vet's partner and sometimes took care of Taz.

"Well, hello, Derrick," she said.

"How's it going?"

"Ah, you know Hannah," Kara said, over the noise of the jukebox. "This is Danita Sanchez and Beth Murphy."

"Looks like you're in good company, son," Derrick said, after nodding a greeting to the others.

Connor blushed.

"I'd say we're the ones in good company," Kara said. "As a matter of fact, I was just about to ask Connor to dance."

"Yeah, right," the boy muttered.

"Come on. Please?"

Connor started to protest more, but Kara overrode him. "No excuses. I'm dying to take a spin on the floor, but I'm sort of rusty." She stood and held out her hand. "You'll have to go slow."

"Like that'll be a problem." Connor wheeled his chair onto the dance floor with as much enthusiasm as an acrophobic who'd been invited to go base jumping.

Fascinated, Derrick kept his gaze locked on Kara. A Lee Ann Womack song about choosing to dance through life played on the jukebox, and Kara leaned over Connor's wheelchair, one hand on his right shoulder, and whispered in his ear. With the other, she took hold of the chair's armrest. Looking sheepish, Connor laced one arm through hers in a way that enabled him to still maneuver the wheelchair.

Kara stepped and twisted slowly to the music, helping Connor spin the chair, guiding it in a circle. Moving with the beat, she stepped forward, then back, keeping Connor beside her at all times in their own modified version of a two-step. To Derrick's delight, Connor said something that made her laugh.

I'll be damned.

It was the first time in—how long?—since he'd seen Connor enjoying himself.

"Pretty good, huh?" Danita said into Derrick's ear.

"Yeah." He wasn't sure if she meant Kara or Connor. Either way, he was impressed.

"Come on," Hannah said. "Let's join them." She grabbed Derrick's hand and tugged him out onto the floor.

He slipped one hand into hers and put the other on her waist, taking the lead. He made sure to keep enough distance from Kara and Connor so as not to embarrass his son. God forbid.

But he was so proud of Connor. *Thank you, Kara.*

As the song ended, a rancher he knew cut in.

Derrick handed Hannah over and tipped his hat, before going to sit down again. Beth and Danita had ordered another round of soft drinks.

A moment later, Kara accompanied Connor back to the table. She gave him a quick bow.

"Thanks, kiddo. You're the best dance partner I've had in a long time."

"Yeah, sure," Connor said. He took a sip of his Coke, hiding his pleasure. "Hey, how about you, Dad?"

"Naw, I don't want to dance with you."

Connor threw a straw at him. "Dork."

"Excuse me, ma'am." A tall, blond cowboy wearing a pair of tight Wranglers and a belt buckle big enough to kill two ducks with one swing tipped his hat to Kara. "Would you care to dance?"

Derrick glared at the guy. To his surprise, Kara shook her head.

"Thanks, anyway," she said. "But I'm taking a breather."

"No problem." The guy turned to Beth. "How about you, pretty lady?"

"Sloppy seconds, huh?"

The man's face reddened. "No, ma'am, I—"

"I'm kidding," Beth said, standing. "Let's go, cowboy."

The guy whirled her out onto the floor. Derrick wished he could have a few minutes alone with Kara, to thank her. "You're a mighty fine dancer," he said, hoping his eyes communicated his gratitude.

"Why, thank you." Her smile said she got it.

Derrick glanced at his watch. Less than ten minutes left of his break. Before he could ask her to dance, the jukebox rang out a popular line dancing song, and Danita grabbed Kara by the hand.

"Come on. You're not sitting this one out. You, too, Hannah."

Kara gave him a "What's a girl to do?" shrug.

"You can join us, Derrick," Danita said.

"Naw, thanks. I've gotta get ready to go back on stage shortly."

He watched as Kara moved out onto the floor, her hands tucked against her trim waist. He couldn't take his eyes off her as she wriggled her cute butt in time to the music. He'd never much cared for line dancing, but maybe there was something to it after all. Kara looked sexy in her jeans, western-cut blouse and boots. With her hair in a French braid, she looked young enough to be carded.

Derrick still had a hard time grasping the fact she was a widow. Widows were supposed to be gray-haired senior citizens. He wondered what her husband had been like. Was he the reason Kara didn't seem interested in dancing with any of the cowboys in the bar? The skinny guy in the spray-on jeans hadn't been the first to ask her.

The line dance ended, and he stood. "You doing all right, son?"

"Yeah."

"Need any more money?"

"I'm good."

"See you next break, then." Derrick paused beside Kara just before she reached the table.

He spoke into her ear. "Thanks for dancing with Connor."

"Are you kidding? He's a great kid."

"Yeah, he is." Derrick fought the urge to stall for time. His band was waiting. "See you in a bit."

"Will do."

Her smile stayed with him the rest of the night.

DERRICK FELL INTO BED, feeling the rewarding sort of exhaustion that always came after a night of performing. A glance at the clock told him he needed to be asleep. The sun would be up in about four hours, and he didn't like sleeping in late when Connor was around. He'd rather be with his son, who'd never been the kind of kid to lie in bed 'til noon.

Derrick stretched out, lacing his hands behind his head on the pillow, letting the late-May breeze coming from the open window wash over him. He took pleasure in knowing that tonight his son slept under his roof and not Shelly's. Still, thoughts of Kara wouldn't let him sleep.

There was something about her that left him curious, wanting to know more.

He knew what it was, making him feel that way—that she'd lost her husband at such a young age. They'd both suffered the trauma of an unexpected accident. She'd lost her husband, and he'd lost the right to be a full-time father.

Derrick wished Shelly would give him more time with their son. Shelly had filled the primary role of raising Connor and that cut him deeply.

No matter.

He laughed dryly and pulled the blanket up over his waist. He was a living country song.

KARA GOT UP EARLY Sunday morning and dressed for church. Her attendance was sporadic, but Liz had phoned two days ago and asked if Kara would join her for this service, it being Memorial Day weekend.

"I'm just not up to driving today," she'd said. "And you know Memorial Day was always so important to Bill."

Evan's father had spent years in the armed forces, and had died from health complications caused by his stint in Vietnam.

When would Liz realize she wasn't the only grieving widow in the family, the only person with needs? But as soon as the thought was out, Kara felt guilty. The least she could do was be there for her mother-in-law, and playing chauffeur was not a lot to ask.

As Kara slipped into her old summer dress, she wondered if she wasn't hoping to atone for her sin of the night before—thinking things about Derrick she had no business thinking. She'd been unable to get him off her mind all night. His voice had sent delicious shivers up her spine.

Being such a huge country music fan, she couldn't believe she was lucky enough to have a neighbor who crooned to her. At least, that's what it had felt like as Derrick sang.

What are you thinking?

Kara cringed.

She reached for her bible, then headed out the door.

Minutes later, she pulled up in front of Liz's modest brick house. To Kara, the place always seemed swallowed by the enormous lawn—something else Kara took care of for her mother-in-law. The riding lawn mower Bill had left behind terrified the older woman.

A whiff of Chanel Number Five preceded Liz into the truck. Kara greeted her, then headed for the small, white-frame church in Sage Bend's four-block downtown.

"Want to get a bite to eat?" Kara asked after the service.

Liz pulled a compact from her purse and checked her coral lipstick. "I don't know...I felt a bit clammy earlier. Do you think I look pale? I was hoping this new lipstick would help put some color in my face." She touched her cheek. "Blush, too."

"You look fine," Kara said.

At fifty-five, Liz was a pretty woman with a curvy figure. Her auburn hair—thick and wavy like Evan's—was cut in a neat low-maintenance bob. Liz was as smart as a whip and, when she put her mind to it, she had a sharp sense of humor. In spite of her neediness, Liz was quite a catch. Kara was sure the many good qualities she saw in her mother-in-law were things men were also bound to notice and find attractive.

Yet Liz had chosen not to remarry. As far as Kara knew, she'd never even dated another man after Bill died.

Suddenly, Kara saw her own reflection in Liz. Would she, too, end up alone for the rest of her life?

Except she wouldn't even have a daughter-in-law to lean on. Just Indio and Lady.

"Kara?"

"Huh?"

"Do I look pale?"

"Oh, no…you don't. Did you take your medication today?"

Liz nodded.

"If you aren't feeling up to lunch, I can take you home and fix you some tea and toast."

"Well, maybe I could manage some soup, or a salad," Liz said. "But there's bound to be a long wait for a table at the diner, this being Sunday."

"True." Kara thought of the steakhouse adjoining the Silver Spur. "We could go for a steak sandwich or something."

"Where?"

"Um, the Silver Spur."

"Oh, Kara." Liz looked at her in a way that made her want to sink into her seat. "That's a *bar*."

"Not on Sundays," Kara said, feeling suddenly defensive. She'd done nothing wrong last night, and there was nothing wrong with having a steak sandwich at the Spur, either. "People take their kids to eat there during the week, too."

"Well," Liz said, clearly pained, "I guess it would be all right." Then she laughed. "Besides, Bill always did like his cold beer."

Bill Tillman hadn't been a churchgoer, though he hadn't been one to hang out in the bars, either. He'd been a boisterous, fun guy who'd felt like a father to Kara, and she missed him something awful. No one could listen to that man laugh and not want to join in.

Minutes later, Kara parked her truck.

And felt her heart stop as she spotted Derrick's pickup.

Had he left it here last night and rode home with his band? Maybe the Chevy wouldn't start or something.

But as Kara reached the side door to the Silver Spur, a step behind Liz, Derrick walked through it on his way out.

"Well, hey there, stranger," he said. "What are you doing back so soon?"

Ignoring Liz's stare, Kara managed a smile. "Just having a bite to eat. I didn't know you worked on Sundays."

"I don't." He held up a fancy guitar pick. "I lost it backstage. Had to come find it. It brings me luck."

"Yeah?" Her brain refused to work.

"You look nice," he added.

She couldn't answer.

"Who's your friend, Kara?" Liz asked, studying Derrick.

Kara found her voice. "I'm sorry. Liz, this is Derrick Mertz—my neighbor. Derrick, my mother-in-law, Liz Tillman."

"Nice to meet you, ma'am."

He even tipped his cowboy hat, but the old-fashioned gesture had no effect on Liz.

She smiled coolly at him. "You play in the band here?"

"That's right."

"I see. Well, we'd better get a table, Kara."

Kara's stomach rolled. She no longer felt hungry.

"See you later, then," Derrick said. He spoke politely, but his eyes fastened on hers in a way that made her wish she could fade into the sidewalk.

"Bye." Hurriedly, she followed Liz inside.

At a table in the dining area, Liz sat across from her, not looking at her open menu. "Kara, what did he mean, 'What are you doing back so soon?'"

"I, um, came here last night to hear Derrick's band. He's the lead singer of Wild Country."

"Isn't that the band you and Evan used to listen to here on occasion?"

Liz's question nearly did her in. "It might've been. I really can't remember."

Liz leaned forward and covered Kara's hand with hers. "Honey, what were you doing in a *bar*— alone—for heaven's sake?"

"I wasn't alone," Kara hedged. "I was with friends."

"Oh?"

"Yes." Kara drew her hand away as unobtrusively as possible. She refused to let Liz make her feel worse than she already did.

She really *hadn't* done anything wrong.

"Well, it still doesn't look right," Liz said. "Kara, I'm old-fashioned enough to know the way of small towns." She sat back in her seat. "Evan's only been gone eight months. People will talk if you're out partying."

"I wasn't partying," Kara said gently. She opened her menu. "I was with the women from my riding club." The half truth came out more easily than she would've thought. "And I drank Coke."

Liz smiled sadly. "I know you're still young, sweetie, and I want you to have fun. I just don't want to see you get hurt. You're at a vulnerable point in your life right now."

"Yes, I am," Kara said. She gave Liz's arm a squeeze. "And that's why I'm so glad I've got you to lean on." No matter what, she'd never let Liz down.

Liz raised one eyebrow. "I think we both know you're full of blarney."

Kara laughed. "Seriously, I don't know what I'd do without you." That much was true. "Now, what looks good?"

Derrick Mertz.

Kara shoved the thought from her mind.

TUESDAY AT THE BANK was crazy busy after the three-day weekend. Kara worked the drive-up window, and the traffic coming through made the morning fly. Things slowed down somewhat after lunch. Just as she served the last car of three, Derrick's silver Chevy S-10 pulled in behind it. Since when had he opened an account here?

Uncomfortable after the chilly brush-off Liz had given him Sunday, Kara pasted a smile on her face as he pulled up to the window.

"Good afternoon," she said through the microphone.

"Hey, there." Derrick smiled back at her and put a deposit slip and check into the window tray. Kara slid it inside.

"I didn't realize you banked with us," she said, not wanting to look at his check or handle the transaction. She shouldn't be privy to how much money he made. But what choice did she have? She could call another teller over, but it would make for an awkward scene.

"I just opened an account here last Friday."

"Oh. I didn't see you. Guess I was out to lunch." When she put Derrick's receipt back in the tray, she noticed he was looking at a poster taped to the inside of her teller booth. It was an ad for an upcoming classic car show, to be held in the parking lot of the local burger joint.

"Are you taking Connor to the car show?"

"No."

Surprised by his abrupt answer, Kara raised her eyebrows. "Why not? I'll bet he'd love it." She remembered how Connor had commented on her truck. "They usually have a lot of cool pickups, not to mention good ol' muscle cars."

Derrick snatched the receipt from the tray. "I said no. See ya."

With that, he pulled away. Kara stared after him.

"What's his problem?" Nadine, a fellow teller asked.

"I have no idea."

But she meant to find out.

A short while later, Kara stood at his front door. It was open, the television tuned to a news program. Derrick sat slumped in a recliner in front of the TV. Kara rapped on the screen, pretending not to look inside.

He saw her and stood. "Hey."

"Hi. May I come in for a minute?"

He opened the screen door with what seemed like reluctance. Puzzled, Kara stepped into the living room.

"Have a seat." Derrick indicated the couch.

"Thank you." She sat perched on the sofa's edge, wondering where Connor was. "Look, I'll get right to the point. If you were short with me today at the bank because my mother-in-law was rude to you yesterday, then—"

"That had nothing to do with it." He turned down the TV's volume with the remote control, then sat on the far end of the couch.

Kara waited, but he offered no further explanation. She couldn't let it go. She felt sorry for Connor.

"So, if you don't want to take Connor to the car show, can I take him?"

"If you want to ask me out, Kara, just do it."

Her jaw literally dropped. "Lord, give a guy a guitar and he thinks he's God's gift." She folded her arms. "I'm asking Connor out, not you."

What had happened to the carefree guy she'd seen at the Silver Spur? A guy who seemed attracted to her.

Derrick glanced in the direction of what Kara assumed was Connor's room. He lowered his voice. "Connor is the reason I said no."

"I don't understand." Kara stared blankly at him.

Derrick nodded toward the side porch. "You want to go outside for a few minutes?"

"Fine." Confused, Kara followed him to the porch. To her surprise, he shut not just the sliding screen, but the glass door as well.

He motioned for her to take a seat, then sat in the chair beside the round patio table. "Kara, I like you a lot," Derrick said. "So, I guess I need to be up front with you." He sighed. "I didn't mean to be rude to you at the bank, or now, either. It's just that...well, me and classic cars don't mix very well anymore."

"What do you mean?"

He took a breath. "It's my fault Connor's in that wheelchair."

"What?" Of all the things she'd expected him to say...

"Yeah." He laced his fingers together, leaning forward in the chair to rest his elbows on his knees. For a long moment, he didn't look up. "On my nineteenth birthday, I took Connor out for a drive. He was two."

Kara couldn't hide her surprise. "My God—you were just a baby when he was born!"

"But I grew up quick." Derrick's eyes darkened. "I had a '68 Ford Gran Torino. My grandpa and I had souped it up, and I was out cruising around, mad at Shelly—Connor's mother—for sticking me with him that night. I let some guy I'd gone to high school with goad me into a drag race."

Kara bit her lip. The sound of birds chirping in the shrubbery seemed like a travesty, in light of Derrick's words.

"I ended up rolling the car. Connor received severe spinal injuries that caused him to be paralyzed from the waist down. All because I was so stupid."

"Dear God." Kara sat, stunned. "Derrick, I don't know what to say…. That must be awfully hard to cope with."

"Yeah. I take it day by day."

She nodded. "What happened to the other boy? Did he wreck, too?"

"No. He drove off and left us in a cow pasture."

Kara sucked in her breath. "You're kidding. Did the police charge him with anything?"

"Leaving the scene of an accident. He got a slap on the wrist, and the boy riding with him got off scot-free," Derrick said bitterly. "They went back to their college dorms that fall, while I faced charges of reckless driving, and the loss of my parental rights."

"Oh, Derrick."

"I had supervised visitation for a long time. Then finally, I got to bring Connor home with me every other weekend. Now he gets to stay two weeks out of four during the summer." He didn't seem to see her, just stared straight ahead at the old tree swing the previous owners left behind. "He's all I've got. My parents are close to Connor, but they don't speak to me. Guess I can't blame them."

Kara fought the urge to hug him. "I'm so sorry."

"Don't feel sorry for me. I did this to my son."

"But thank God your son is alive."

"Believe me, I do. Every day."

Kara wished she could find the words to make Derrick feel better. To help him see that Connor's life was still one to be treasured and lived to the fullest, not something to think of as screwed up. She'd give anything to have Evan here with her, even in a wheelchair.

Suddenly, she felt angry. "Maybe the car show would be a reminder to you that you caused your son pain." She stood. "But maybe for Connor, it would simply be an afternoon doing something fun with his father. He can't remember the accident anyway."

Derrick scowled. "I suppose not."

"Not just because he was two," Kara said, "but because he told me so."

His face blanched. "Connor told you about the accident?"

"No. He said he'd been in an accident he couldn't remember—one that had put him in a wheelchair. Doesn't he know what happened?"

"Of course. As soon as he was old enough to understand, I told him."

"Connor also told me I had a sweet-looking truck. That's why I think you should let him go to the car show."

"I said no."

"You're being selfish!" Her sharp words set the neighbor's dog barking.

Derrick's frown deepened. "You have no right to judge me. You don't know what I've been through…what Connor has been through."

"Maybe not, but if I could have Evan back—" her voice trembled, and Kara fought hard to control it "—I would cherish every last moment with him."

She hurried around the corner of the porch, down the steps, then ran across the street.

CONNOR SAT IN THE DOORWAY between the kitchen and the living room, myriad emotions running through him. His dad had closed the sliding glass door, thinking he wouldn't be able to hear what he and Kara were arguing about. But the kitchen window was open.

Connor had been in his room on the computer, when he'd heard Kara's voice.

He wished he hadn't listened. He hated the way his dad treated him like a friggin' invalid. Oh, sure, he was handicapped all right, stuck in this damned chair for the rest of his life. But that didn't make him an invalid—weak.

If only he could get his dad to see him as a regular kid, even if he himself did not. It was all he'd ever wanted. He hated the heavy guilt his father carried…for all these years. He may not remember the accident, but Connor knew every detail. He'd lived it through what his dad told him about the wreck, and from that, he had a pretty good picture of what his dad had been through.

Connor shared his dad's guilt, since he was the cause of it. If he'd never been born, his dad wouldn't have to live with that. Some days, he wished he *hadn't* been born. Some days he wished he'd just go to sleep and never wake up. He was sick of this freakin' chair, sick of not being able to do things his classmates did, and most of all, he was sick of pretending he was okay with it.

What would it feel like to be *normal?* His school counselor hated it when he used that word. She'd told him no one was normal and that just because he was confined to a wheelchair didn't make him any less a person.

Bullshit.

He'd give anything to ride bulls the way John Brody did, or play soccer like Kevin. And knowing he'd never have a girlfriend really sucked big-time, especially now that his hormones had kicked in. He might be partially paralyzed, but he still had feelings. Connor envied the guys at school who had girlfriends. Some of the guys weren't even virgins anymore.

And here he'd never even kissed a girl. Not really. There'd been that one time when he was nine, and Amy Broderick had kissed him on a dare. But that was it. One humiliating kiss. His life sucked, and now his dad couldn't even let him go to a damned car show.

Shaking his head in disgust, Connor wheeled back to his room and closed the door. He signed back into the chat room as BullRider85.

Hey ColoradoCowgirl. You still there?

Yep. Where'd u go?

2 the kitchen 2 get a beer, Connor typed.

It must be rad to be 21 and have your own place. Are you really a cowboy?

You'd better know it. I won a 1st place trophy

buckle in the college finals last year. But I busted up my leg 2 bad 2 ride for a while.

Aw...want me to kiss it and make it better?

Now you're talking.

Connor grinned, his gaze locked on the computer screen.

This was where ColoradoCowgirl, who said she was eighteen, usually started making things really interesting.

He read her next message and continued to type, ignoring his dad's rule against chat rooms. E-mail only worked if you had someone to write to, and besides Kevin, Connor didn't have many e-pals.

But ColoradoCowgirl made up for that.

He'd risk getting caught by his dad, just to spend one more hour with her.

She made him feel good.

And as BullRider85, he could be anything he wanted to be.

CHAPTER FIVE

June

THE HEATED WORDS he'd had with Kara stuck in Derrick's craw all week, like irritating grains of sand. Not only had he managed to alienate the one woman he'd taken an interest in, but Connor had been quiet and sullen all week, barely talking to him. Still, Derrick phoned home during his shifts bartending at the Spur, to check on his son.

While his days off varied, Derrick generally worked the bar Monday through Friday, 6:30 p.m. to 2:00 a.m.—unless Wild Country was playing. But on the weeks when he had Connor, Tina rearranged the schedule so he could be home no later than seven. He liked to check in with Connor at least once in the evening, to make sure everything was okay. As often as possible, Derrick went home for lunch, but he still worried.

What if Connor fell out of his chair? What if there was a fire and he couldn't get out of the house fast enough? In an emergency, Connor had the phone number of a couple of neighbors who also kept an eye on him. Plus Shelly lived and worked just a few miles away.

The idea of asking Kara to be an emergency contact had crossed Derrick's mind, but she probably wasn't speaking to him, either. He could deal with that from her, but not from his son. In just eight short days, it would be time for Connor to head back to Shelly's.

Derrick arrived home at seven-fifteen on Thursday and found Connor watching television, munching on a bag of cheese puffs. Beside him on the coffee table was a can of Mountain Dew.

"Hey, bud. Did you eat some supper?"

"I had a sandwich." Connor barely glanced his way, his focus on the reality show he was watching.

Derrick picked up the remote control, which was covered with sticky, cheese-dust fingerprints, and switched it off.

"Hey, I was watching that!"

Now he had the boy's attention. "We need to talk," Derrick said, laying the remote on the coffee table.

"About what?" Connor sulked, slumping in his chair.

"What's gotten into you this week? Have I done something to make you mad?"

Connor gave him a look that said he was dense. "Gee, I don't know, Dad. Maybe if you think about it, you'll figure it out." He grabbed for the remote, but Derrick moved it out of reach.

"Leave the TV off." He stared at Connor. "What's the matter?"

Connor mumbled an expletive, but Derrick let it slide.

"I'm tired of all this crap," Connor said. "Tired of this damned chair, and tired of having you treat me like I'm ten."

Derrick felt as if the wind had been knocked out of him. "What are you talking about, son? Would I take a ten-year-old to the spur? I thought you had a fun time the other night, with me and Kara and her friends."

"It was okay."

"And what about our Friday night burgers, and hanging out with the band? If that's not an adult thing to do, I don't know what is."

"That's great, Dad. But you just don't get it."

"Explain it to me, then."

"I heard what you said to Kara about the car show." He set his jaw. "I want to go."

Derrick's gut began to churn. "Why didn't you just tell me?"

"You think everything is bad for me, or beyond my capabilities, which of course, most things are."

He gestured angrily, his voice rising on a note of sarcasm. "Ol' cripple boy can't make the rodeo team or go to the prom. But he can manage a pity spin on the dance floor at the Spur with his dad's girlfriend!"

"She's not my girlfriend, and she didn't dance with you out of pity." Derrick wasn't sure whether to be angry or sad. He'd had no idea his son had grown this bitter.

"You know, Dad," Connor went on, "what makes it worse is that you won't stop blaming yourself for what happened to me. I hate that."

Dumbstruck, Derrick blinked. "I—yeah, I blame myself. It was my fault. There's no way around that, and it's something I'll never get over. I can't tell you how sorry I am that I was so damned stupid."

"Why? Because I'm not good enough the way I am?"

"God, no!" Connor's words cut like a razor. "That couldn't be further from the truth."

"No? Then why do you treat me the way you do? I can't go to a stupid car show because it might remind me of how screwed up I am? Isn't that what you said to Kara?"

"No, that's not what I meant at all. Son—"

"Don't bother," Connor said, thrusting his wheelchair away from the coffee table. "I don't want to go to the damned thing now anyway!" He spun the chair around and wheeled angrily toward his room.

"Connor, come back here." Derrick stubbed his toe on the coffee table, but barely felt it through his cowboy boot. He did, however, jostle the table enough to spill the can of pop. It flowed in a yellow puddle toward the remote control, and Derrick made a wild grab for it. He tossed the remote on the couch, and righted the can, leaving the mess to clean up later.

"Connor!" He hurried down the hall, but Connor slammed the door shut and locked it before Derrick could reach him. "Son, open the door. We need to talk."

"Leave me alone."

Derrick sighed, leaning his forehead against the doorjamb. He clenched his fist and pressed it to the headache that was beginning to throb at his temples. He'd thought things were going more smoothly. Now he'd messed up whatever progress he'd made with his son by being overprotective. By looking out for his own wants and needs instead of paying closer attention to exactly what Connor wanted.

Kara had been right. He was the one who didn't want to face the car show and the memories it would bring.

"Connor, I was wrong. Come on, open the door."

Silence.

"You can go to the car show. I—I'll even go with you." It would be tough, but if that's what it took to make things right with his son…

"I said I don't want to go."

"Fine. Then let's do something else. This is our last weekend for a while."

Connor responded by cranking up his stereo, and the music of Big and Rich boomed off the walls. Derrick started to shout at him to turn it down. But what good would it do? Instead, he slammed his fist against the wall, then turned and walked away.

SATURDAY'S WEATHER FORECAST called for the temperature to reach the high eighties, so Kara met Danita, Beth and Hannah at the stables bright and early. They had their horses saddled and were on the trail by six-thirty. Kara breathed in the pine-scented air, letting the bird calls soothe away her tension, as Indio walked briskly along with Lady at her heels.

"So, Kara, do you want to go to the Silver Spur with us tonight?" Hannah asked. "I'll bet Derrick's playing."

"I don't think so," Kara said. "He told me he only plays most Fridays and every other Saturday."

"Do you mean 'I don't think so' as in you don't want to go," Beth said, "or as in you don't think Derrick is playing?"

Kara laughed. "Both, actually." She couldn't forget the way Liz had looked at her when they'd run into Derrick last Sunday. Plus, she hadn't talked to him since their argument. She felt bad about it, once she'd gotten over her initial anger. Derrick was right.

If he didn't want to take his son there, it was his business.

"Now, that's a cop-out," Danita said, interrupting her thoughts. "You had fun last weekend, and you know it. What does it matter if Derrick's playing or not? If he isn't, invite him along! This is a family night Saturday, I think."

"It *doesn't* matter," Kara said, "and I don't want to invite him."

Danita glared at her. "I thought we'd been over this before."

"You're one to talk," Kara shot back. "I still haven't seen you dating the fire chief."

"Hey, I danced with plenty of men the other night," Danita said. "I don't need the fire chief."

"I don't know," Hannah teased. "From what I remember, Shawn Rutherford is pretty darned good-looking."

"Yeah, well so is Derrick Mertz," Danita said. "Come on, Kara. Ask him out."

"No!"

"Why?" all three of her friends asked as one.

Kara nudged Indio over, pretending to crowd Danita off the trail. Danita good-naturedly pushed at Kara's stirrup with her booted toe. "Get back, girl, or I'll have to hurt you."

"Hey, you're just cranky because you haven't had enough coffee yet." Kara smiled, wishing her friends would forget about Derrick and talk about something or someone else.

"No," Danita said. "I'm cranky because Phillip had the nerve to call last night and see if I could look for a tie tack he thinks he might've dropped behind the dresser. He probably has a hot date with his slut. As if I'd help him look good for it."

"I don't think he'd wear a suit on a date," Hannah said. "Would he?" Then she cringed at the look on Danita's face. "Sorry."

"It doesn't matter what he'd wear when," Beth added, looking over her shoulder at them as Sundance pushed past Ricochet. "He's a scum-sucking pig, and I hope he gets food poisoning the next time he takes his bimbo out."

"Come on, Beth, you can do better than that," Hannah said. "He deserves a far worse fate. Like rat poison. Wouldn't you love to feed him some, Danita? And that woman, too?"

"He's not worth the jail time," Danita scoffed. "Besides, he's probably boinked every woman in his clinic. I'd have to poison a lot of food."

"Nah," Hannah said. "Melanie Spencer wouldn't sleep with him. I know her better than that."

"You know Melanie?" Danita asked.

"I take care of her horses. She runs a therapeutic riding center, you know."

"She does?" Kara's ears perked.

"She works at the massage clinic three days a week," Hannah said, "and the rest of the time she works with handicapped kids at her ranch, giving therapeutic riding lessons."

"That's right," Danita said. "Hey, Kara, are you thinking about Connor?"

"Yeah, actually I am," Kara said.

It might be a way to set things right with Derrick. He seemed to like horses, from the conversation they'd had the day he carried her tack to her truck. And Connor had told her he liked horses, too.

The idea was perfect.

"Can you give me Melanie's phone number, Danita? Hannah?"

"Sure." Danita shrugged. "Or you can look her up in the book. Her riding center is called God's Little Acre."

"I've driven past it," Kara said. "But I didn't realize the ranch was a therapeutic riding center."

"Melanie's real sweet, too," Danita went on. "I ran into her at the grocery store the other day. She was very sympathetic about what Phillip did to me. At least she took my side over his, even though they work together."

Hannah chuckled. "Just because she works out of the same clinic doesn't mean she isn't smart."

"I'll tell you who isn't smart," Danita said, "and that's the bimbo girlfriend. Just wait until she finds out what Phillip's really like. He's addicted to watching sports and those nasty-looking Vienna sausage things...."

Kara let her attention wander. She'd call Melanie today after she got back from her ride, and ask about visiting the riding center. Then she'd talk to Derrick and see if he and Connor were interested in going. Maybe she should talk to Derrick alone, not in front of Connor, in case he got upset with her again. She didn't want to make any assumptions this time, even though she was pretty sure he'd be happy about the therapeutic riding. She still wished he'd reconsider the car show.

Reminding herself again that it was Derrick's business what he did or didn't let his son do, Kara urged Indio into a lope as her friends picked up the pace.

Up ahead, Lady had veered off the trail to wade in the creek alongside of it.

"Hey, does anybody want to race?" Kara challenged. "There's a straightaway coming up around the next bend. Last one to the blue spruce that was struck by lightning buys drinks at the Silver Spur."

"Then you're coming with us tonight?" Beth asked.

Why not? She couldn't very well hide from Derrick if she was going to help Connor.

"I suppose."

"All right!" Hannah said, giving Ricochet free rein. "You're on!"

"Ya-hoo!" Beth shouted, leaning low over Sundance's neck as the mare sprang into a run.

Kara let Indio take off in a burst of speed, the wind rushing against her. Exhilarated, she welcomed it. "Come on, Indio!" she shouted. "Yee-haw!"

CHAPTER SIX

DERRICK MANAGED TO TALK Connor into going out for a burger Saturday afternoon, since he'd ended up having to work late on Friday. Yet when they got home, Connor headed back to his room, and the computer.

Deciding some progress was better than none at all, Derrick left him alone. In the kitchen, he started putting away the breakfast dishes Connor had washed earlier, but when he opened the cupboard, he saw the blue plastic pitcher that belonged to Kara. He'd forgotten to return it once he and Connor finished off the lemonade. It was a handy excuse to go over to her house and make nice, so Derrick headed out the door.

Her truck had been gone earlier when he and Connor went to town, but it was back now. On the porch, Derrick raised his hand to rap on the screen door, but Kara appeared at that exact moment.

"Derrick." She looked startled to find him standing there. "I was just heading over to your house."

"Really?" He studied her face, trying to read her expression.

From the fenced backyard, her collie dog ran up to the chain link and barked at him. "Hey, Lady," he called. "How'd you get so muddy?"

"She waded through the creek while I was out riding this morning. She's going to have to have a bath before she can come back in the house." Kara held the screen door open. "Come on in."

"I thought I'd better return your lemonade pitcher." Derrick held it aloft as he stepped inside.

"Oh, thanks." Kara took it, then motioned for him to sit down. "I'll be right back."

Derrick started to sit in a comfortable-looking leather chair, but his gaze fell on the photo on top of the entertainment center. Kara in her wedding gown—looking too young to be a bride—clinging happily to the arm of her husband. Curious, Derrick took a closer look.

What had she said his name was? Edwin…no Evan. That was it. In the photo, Evan Tillman looked like the happiest guy on earth. And who could blame him, with Kara on his arm? She was gorgeous in the lacy bridal gown, the scooped neckline showing a hint of cleavage. Her hair had been even longer then, and it lay draped over her shoulder like so much silk.

Derrick picked up the photo and studied Evan. The guy wasn't bad-looking. He had reddish-brown hair, cut neat, and he was dressed in a gray, western-style tux and cowboy boots.

So, Kara had a thing for cowboys.

Or at least one.

"Would you like something to drink?" Kara called from the kitchen.

Starting guiltily, Derrick almost dropped the picture. "Yeah, sure. Whatever you've got handy."

Quickly, he set it back in place and dropped into the leather chair. Signs of Evan's presence seemed to jump out at him everywhere. A hardhat hung from a row of wooden pegs behind the front door, and an open coat closet revealed a pair of men's work boots on the floor. More pictures of Kara and Evan lined the walls, and in one corner of the room was a gun rack, a lever-action Winchester—probably a .30-.30—hanging on it. The rifle looked well-used but lovingly cared for.

"I hope Diet Pepsi is all right," Kara said. "It's about all I've got right now, unless you want more pink—"

Caught staring at her dead husband's rifle, Derrick forced a smile and reached for the can. "That's fine, thanks."

Kara quickly hid her expression—but not quickly enough. And suddenly, it hit Derrick between the eyes. She was still in love with the guy. Not that he'd expected her to be over him after only a few months, but…

But what?

Derrick popped the tab and took a healthy swig, determined to keep this visit short.

"I didn't come over just to return your lemonade pitcher," he said.

"No?"

"I wanted to say I'm sorry for being so hard on you the other day. It's just that what happened to Connor is still something I have a real tough time dealing with, obviously."

"Say no more." Kara held up a hand. "I completely understand. And for the record, I was on my way over to apologize as well."

"Is that right?" This time his smile was genuine.

"I shouldn't have butted in where Connor is concerned. Which is why I'm not so sure you're going to like what I'm about to suggest."

"What's that?"

She fiddled nervously with her pop tab. "I know someone who gives therapeutic riding lessons to handicapped kids. That is, my friends know her. Melanie Spencer."

"I've heard about her riding center."

"Really?"

He nodded. But for some reason, he'd never considered taking Connor there.

"I was thinking Connor might want to go there. I know where the center is, if you think he might like to check it out."

Derrick had pictured the place as somewhere that severely disabled children went to exercise their motor skills. Connor already had a physical therapist. Shelly had chosen the guy.

"That's nice of you to think of him, Kara, but I don't know." He shrugged. "Connor likes horses, but he's never really been around them much. I used to have one when I was young, and my parents..." He didn't want to get into details about his estrangement from them. "My folks have a place over by Miles City. They still have a couple of horses, but I don't think they ride them much anymore." Not from what Connor had told him.

"Well, you could ask him if he'd like to..."

"Mmm-hmm." He studied her. Why had she taken such an interest in his son? The other day, he'd accused her of using Connor to get close to him. Women had tried that before. But at the same time, Kara was the only woman who seemed to genuinely see past Connor's wheelchair and relate to the boy.

"That is, if you want to," Kara hastened to add. "I'm not trying to be nosy again. It was just something that came up today while I was out riding with my friends."

"I didn't think you were being nosy," Derrick said. "But honestly, Kara, I have to ask—why so much interest in my son?"

Obviously, she and Evan hadn't had any kids.

And obviously they'd been married long enough, by the looks of the wedding photo.

Connor already had a mom. He didn't need another one.

Kara's pretty, freckled skin flushed a pale pink. "I like Connor," she said. "As I said before, he's a good kid."

"He is. And Shelly is a good mother. Connor's not lacking for parental guidance." He kept his tone soft, not wanting to hurt her feelings.

She blushed even deeper. "I wasn't insinuating anything of the sort," she said. "It's just that I couldn't help but notice he doesn't seem to have any friends to hang out with. I thought maybe the riding center might be a place where he could meet a few."

"Kids like him?"

"Well, yeah." She lifted a shoulder. "Just kids, you know? Someone he can laugh and talk with besides a bunch of adults in a bar."

Her comment made him bristle. "Are you saying I'm a bad influence, letting my boy hang out in a honky-tonk?"

"No!" Kara set her Diet Pepsi down with a bang. "For heaven's sake, Derrick. Are you always so defensive? I'm only trying to help."

"Fine." He had no idea what riding lessons cost, but if Connor were interested, Derrick would find a way to pay for them. "We can ask him."

"Really?"

"Yeah, really." He stood, feeling the sudden need to get out of this room and away from Evan's ghost. "You want to come on over to my place, or would you rather I asked Connor?"

"No, I'll go with you. I like chatting with him." She stood as well. "As a matter of fact, I was wondering if the two of you were going to be at the Silver Spur tonight? Danita's going there with Beth and Hannah again, and they invited me along."

"Are you asking me out, Kara?" This time his tone was teasing, making a mockery of his own pissy attitude toward her the other day.

"No. Well, yeah. I guess I am."

He laughed. "I'm not playing with my band tonight, or bartending, either. I'd thought I might take Connor to a movie or something, but I can see what he wants to do."

"Oh, gosh—don't let me interfere with your movie plans." She tucked her hands in her back pockets. "Really, it's no big deal."

But suddenly, it was a big deal to him. Kara was actually asking him out.

"Come on." He nodded toward the front door. "Let's go on over and talk to Connor. See what he thinks about everything."

He stepped aside, letting her pass through the door first.

But before he closed it behind them, his gaze fell on the Winchester rifle again. It hung there, like a silent threat left behind by Evan.

Stay away from my wife.

WHAT HAD SHE BEEN THINKING, asking Derrick to go to the Silver Spur? Somehow, the invitation had tumbled out before she could stop it. Danita would never let her live it down.

"Connor," Derrick called as they stepped into the living room. He walked down the hallway to rap on Connor's bedroom door. "Kara's here. Come on out a minute."

Kara heard the door open, then the sound of quiet arguing. She made out the words "chat room" and "I told you." Connor's reply was inaudible, but he sounded upset. Maybe this hadn't been such a swift idea after all. But she was already here. She couldn't very well walk out.

A moment later, Connor came wheeling down the hallway. "Hi, Kara," he said, looking sullen.

"Hey, Connor." She smiled, hesitant. "I wanted to ask you and your dad to the Silver Spur tonight, but he tells me you might go to a movie."

"I don't know." Connor shrugged, not looking at Derrick.

Kara plowed ahead. "Also, I was wondering if you might be interested in horseback riding?"

"Riding?" He looked at her, frowning. But his eyes sparkled with interest. "Me?"

"Sure. Why not? I know of a therapeutic riding center where the horses are specially trained for people with physical challenges—"

"You're talking about that place where the retarded kids ride," Connor accused. "I'm not retarded, and I'm not going to ride with a bunch of little kids."

"Connor!" Derrick pushed away from the wall he'd been leaning against.

"It's okay, Derrick." Kara held up a hand. The boy had likely used the hateful word to rile his dad. "I think you've gotten the wrong impression, Connor. Hannah knows the woman who owns the place, and yes, a lot of the kids are young, and a lot of them have special needs. But there are all sorts of special needs. Why shouldn't you get to ride, too?"

"How?" He gave a sarcastic snort, and indicated his legs. "It would be sort of hard to balance in the saddle."

"They have tack designed so you can, Hannah tells me. And helpers to aid the riders."

"You mean they have people who walk beside the horses while they go in a circle," Connor scoffed. "No thanks. I'm too old for a merry-go-round."

"Enough with the attitude." Derrick folded his arms and took a step closer to Connor. "Kara's just trying to be nice and find a way for you to have fun.

You don't need to be on that damned computer every waking minute of the day."

"Well, excuse me, Dad! You try sitting in a chair twenty-four-seven, and see how bored you get." Connor took off through the kitchen, out the sliding glass doors to the side porch.

"I know he's your kid, Derrick, Kara said, "but could you give me a minute with him?"

Derrick raked a hand through his hair. "Have at it."

"Thanks."

Connor sat at the far end of the porch, staring off into the distance.

"Hey, Connor." Kara pulled up a chair. "I didn't mean to upset you. I'm sorry."

He shrugged, but said nothing.

"Your dad is trying hard. Can't you give him a break?"

The boy's blue eyes met hers, looking so much like Derrick's. "He needs to give *me* a break. I'm not a baby."

"So stop acting like one."

"What?" His eyebrows arched.

"You heard me. You're making your father feel bad, acting this way. If you don't want to ride, that's fine. Why don't you think of something to do your dad won't have a problem with?" She lowered her voice. "You could pick a little guitar with him."

"No!" The answer came out sharp and quick, and

Connor looked as upset as he'd been that day she'd found him playing Derrick's guitar.

"Why not?"

His sullen expression was back. "He doesn't know I play."

Now it was Kara's turn to raise an eyebrow. "He doesn't?"

"And I don't want him to know."

"I don't understand."

Connor sighed. "It's complicated. I don't want to talk about it."

"Okay." Kara stood. "But I sure wish you'd change your mind about God's Little Acre. If you do, let me know." She walked back into the house.

Inside, Derrick looked expectantly at her. "No luck. Sorry." She forced a smile. "But I'd still like to see you guys tonight, if you think Connor will come."

Or come by yourself, so I can spend time with you.

The thought appealed to her more than she cared to admit.

"Thanks," Derrick said. "I guess I'll have to see what's going on."

"Sure." She moved to the front door. "See you later."

"Kara, wait."

She paused, with the screen partway open. "Yeah?"

"I'd like to see the riding center sometime."

"Really?"

Derrick nodded. "Connor will be going to his mom's house next weekend for a couple of weeks. Maybe you could introduce me to Melanie."

Kara started to say that she hadn't met her yet, either. But she felt bad for him. He was trying so hard with his son. It had to be hard enough to parent a teenager without Connor's added challenges.

"Yeah, sure. We can do that. Just let me know exactly when you want to go. I'm off on Saturdays."

"Great. I'll be in touch."

Kara crossed the street, making a beeline for her backyard. She'd wash Lady off with the hose and the dog shampoo she kept in the garage.

That would give her something to keep her mind occupied.

CONNOR SAT ALONE on the porch, waiting for his dad to come outside once Kara left and start yelling at him again for being online in a chat room.

What the hell did his dad think he was going to do? Be stupid enough to give some pervert his address? He knew pedophiles posed as kids online. Just because he couldn't walk didn't mean he was stupid.

Which was the way most of the kids at school treated him. He'd recently found a chat group made up of kids who lived in Montana. In this chat room, he could be himself—ConMan1, a screen name his friends knew him by. Or he could be MTcwby89— an upcoming senior, who'd just moved to the area.

The kids in the group talked about rodeos and country music. And just before his dad had barged in and gone ballistic, Connor saw he'd gotten a reply from a screen name he recognized. CanChaser1. He'd not only run across her in another chat room, but he'd also seen her in town plenty of times—the nickname "Can Chaser" etched across the back window of her fancy Dodge pickup.

Kerri Hendricks. He'd be going to the same high school as her this fall, and her dad owned one of the biggest cattle ranches in Sage Bend. Kerri had been rodeo queen of the county fair last year. She was a top-notch barrel racer, and so damned pretty she made Connor lightheaded every time he saw her. She had long blond hair and brown eyes, and round, full boobs.

But like the girls at his old school, Kerri looked right past him. When he was in the chat room, though, he could talk to her. He was MTcwby89— athletic, good-looking… He'd found a picture of some cowboy on a high school rodeo team in Wyoming and downloaded it to his computer. Then he'd e-mailed it to Kerri. She'd sent her own picture back and flirted with him online. They'd begun to chat on a regular basis.

He'd forgotten all about ColoradoCowgirl.

"Connor."

"What?" Startled, he turned to look over his shoulder.

"We need to talk, son."

Here it came.

"Fine. But can we do it over a pizza? I'm hungry."

To his surprise, his dad smiled. "Yeah, I'll call Piper's and have 'em bring it. We can eat out here on the porch if you want."

"Yeah, sure." Out of the corner of his eye, Connor spotted Kevin heading his way on his BMX bike. Maybe that would hold off his dad's lecture, for a while anyway. "Better get a couple of large ones, Dad. Here comes Kevin."

"Pepperoni?"

"And pineapple."

"All right." His dad paused with one hand on the sliding door. "We're still going to talk. Later."

"Yeah." Connor sighed. "I figured as much."

CHAPTER SEVEN

KARA HAD AN ENJOYABLE EVENING out at the Silver Spur, line dancing and drinking a couple of beers, but she couldn't help feeling disappointed when Derrick failed to show. Considering the difficult time he'd had with Connor earlier, it shouldn't surprise her that he'd chosen to spend time with his son. They'd probably gone to the movies.

Still, every time a new group of people came through the front door, Kara caught herself looking over her shoulder.

"Looking for a certain cowboy?" Danita teased, speaking near her ear to be heard over the country-rock band.

"What if I am?" Kara smirked.

"Hey, you're the one who keeps nagging me about Shawn."

"You should've brought him with you tonight."

Danita wagged a finger at her. "Don't change the subject. We're talking about you and Derrick."

Suddenly, Danita saw something over Kara's shoulder. "Oh, my gosh. Look who just walked in."

Kara quickly turned, fully expecting to see Derrick. Or maybe Shawn Rutherford. To her shock, Liz walked hesitantly into the room, her eyes scanning the crowd. She wore white jeans, cowboy boots and a sage-green western shirt.

"What is Liz doing here?" Hannah asked.

"I can't imagine." Kara rose and worked her way through the crowd.

Liz's eyes lit up when she spotted her.

"Kara. I thought I might find you here."

"My God—Liz. Is something wrong?" She caught her mother-in-law by the elbow and led her over to a quieter corner in the back of the bar, near the restrooms. "Are you sick?"

Liz looked insulted. "No. Are you saying I can't venture out alone?"

"No, it's just that…I thought you hadn't been feeling well lately."

"I decided fresh air might do me some good."

"In this smoky bar?"

Liz had the good grace to blush. "I drove to your house, thinking we might do something together, but since you weren't there, well…"

Pointedly, Kara eyed Liz's western attire. "You thought you'd put on some western clothes and play cowgirl?"

"Now you're making fun of me."

"I'm not." Kara chuckled. "You don't know how good it is to see you here."

"Really? You're not mad?"

"Why would I be?"

Liz squirmed. "You caught me. I *was* checking up on you. I wanted to see the place you've been hanging out at."

Enough to get up the gumption to come to the bar.

"I don't 'hang out' here. I come here once in awhile to hear the music and have fun with my girl-friends."

Her mother-in-law's gaze darted toward the band-stand, even though they didn't have a clear view of it from where they stood. "Is your friend Derrick playing tonight?"

"No. He's not. And that's exactly what he is—a friend." The half truth made Kara feel guilty. But how could she even think about moving on to some-thing more with Derrick, especially seeing the look on Liz's face?

Though she tried to hide it, Liz was clearly relieved and satisfied. "Well. I guess you think I'm horrible, coming here to a bar by myself after I gave you such a hard time."

"Not at all."

"I wasn't going to stay if you weren't here."

Kara read the mixed message. In truth, Liz

would've left if she hadn't found her. On the other hand, since she had...

"Would you like to join me and my friends?" Kara asked. "I know you've met Danita and Hannah, but I don't think you've met Beth yet."

"I'd love to." Brightening, Liz followed her back to the table.

A short while later, she laid her hand on Kara's arm. "Am I crazy, or is that Myrna Shaw sitting at that table over there?" Discreetly, Liz pointed.

Myrna was a prominent member of Liz's church, and sang in the choir.

"It is."

"Dear Lord." Liz clasped one hand to her breast, looking horrified. "What is Myrna doing in a *bar,* for heaven's sake? Have you seen her here before?"

The serious look on her mother-in-law's face caused Kara to bite down on the inside of her bottom lip. Hard. "Um. No, actually, I haven't."

"Don't stare. She'll see us." But Liz snuck another glance over her shoulder. "I can't believe that. And look who's with her. It's Violet Harper!" Liz's jaw dropped. "Violet is a member of Mothers Against Drunk Driving."

Kara shrugged. "That doesn't mean she can't drink. It just means she can't drink and drive."

"Well, for Pete's sake." Liz leaned close. "Come on. Let's go get a Coke at the bar and see who else is here."

KARA GOT OFF WORK at five-thirty the following Friday and drove home, exhausted. She'd picked up some food at the drive-thru window of Taco Johns, and had just sat down to eat in front of the TV when the phone rang.

"Hi." It was Derrick.

Kara's pulse quickened. "Hey. What's up?"

"I talked to Melanie, and I'm going to take a drive out to God's Little Acre tomorrow morning. Still want to come with me?"

"Um, sure. What time?"

"Ten-thirty. That way I can sleep in. I'm playing at the Spur tonight."

Kara laughed. "I would've thought musicians slept in 'til noon."

He chuckled. "I never sleep past nine. That way I've got plenty of time for Connor when he's here."

She loved that he was so devoted to his son. "Ten-thirty it is, then."

"So, are you going to be there tonight?"

"I don't think so," she said. "I'm kind of tired."

Besides, what if Liz showed up again like last Saturday? Even though her mother-in-law had ended up enjoying herself more than Kara would've ever expected, she'd also managed to make Kara feel guilty for being at the honky-tonk.

"Long day at the bank, huh?"

"Yeah."

"Well, I won't keep you then. See you tomorrow."

"Bye." Kara hung up and went back to the table.

But the tacos she'd looked forward to were all but tasteless as she bit into one. Why did Liz get to her?

Kara fed Lady a bite of cheese and ground beef. Kara already knew she wasn't ready for a relationship. Still, that didn't mean she couldn't enjoy Derrick's company. She was tired of being alone.

The next morning, Derrick came to her door promptly at ten-thirty, dressed in blue jeans and a dark blue T-shirt. He wore his hat, which made him look one-hundred-percent cowboy.

"'Morning," he said. "Ready to go?"

"Yep." She closed the door behind her.

It felt strange to ride in Derrick's truck. To be in a vehicle—for the first time in as long as she could remember—with a man who wasn't her husband or her father-in-law or her dad. Kara covered her nervousness with idle chitchat, relieved when they arrived at the riding center.

An Australian shepherd and a spotted dog that looked as if Mother Nature had been unable to decide if he should be a spitz or a dalmatian, trotted alongside the pickup truck, barking. Their noisy welcome drew a woman out of the stables. She was tall with a somewhat masculine build, her salt-and-pepper hair cut short. Her round face creased with laugh lines, her brown skin showed she spent a good deal of time outdoors.

"Hello. You must be Kara and Derrick."

"It's nice to meet you," Kara said as she got out of the truck.

Derrick shook Melanie's hand. "Thanks for taking the time to meet with us." His gaze combed the area.

"You're more than welcome." Melanie motioned them forward. "Come on. I'll give you the grand tour." She chatted as they walked, asking Derrick a few questions about Connor. "I'm sure he'd fit in with our other riders quite nicely. Classes are held five days a week—Monday through Wednesday, and Friday and Saturday. We have several groups, some made up of younger kids, some older—mostly eleven- and twelve-year-olds."

"I'm glad to hear that," Derrick said. "Connor was reluctant to ride with little kids."

"I understand." Melanie gave them a genuinely warm smile. "He's at that age…not a boy, yet not quite grown. My son gave me fits when he was fourteen."

Derrick nodded. "Tell me about it."

Kara looked around, admiring the stables. The barn was freshly painted, white with green trim. It was built in an L-shape, with five stall doors on one side, four on the other. White-fenced paddocks surrounded the building, and the pasture stretched out back of the stables, several horses grazing in the distance. The barn wasn't new, but everything looked well-kept and clean.

"I've got the horses turned out for the day," Melanie said as they went in. "We had early lessons this morning. But they'll come to us easily enough. Let me show you the rest of the facilities first. We've got both indoor and outdoor arenas."

She took them past a large indoor arena to the tack room, and explained the intricacies of the specialized equipment that allowed physically challenged children to stay safely in place.

"We have several trained volunteers and two riding instructors, who work with me in helping the kids with their therapy and lessons," Melanie said. "Initially, a student has three volunteers with him at all times. One to lead the horse, and two—side-walkers—to make sure the rider is safe and secure."

The therapeutic saddles had an extra support element for the rider's back and a large, easy to grasp handle on the front. The students all wore a walker belt, with handholds on either side for the volunteers to grip.

"Once a student can demonstrate complete control of the horse, depending on the limitations of his disability, of course, then we remove the leader and the side-walkers. We also have a thirteen-year-old girl—Lisa Owens—who rides with the students regularly. She acts as a sort of combination volunteer and cheerleader." Melanie smiled. "Some of the children need extra praise and encouragement from someone closer to their own age than us old geezers."

Behind the stables was a round pen and another large arena, with bleachers for parents to sit and watch their children ride. There was also a mounting ramp.

"Tell me more about the specifics of the riding," Derrick said, leaning with one foot propped against the round pen's railing. "What's a typical session?"

"There really isn't a typical session, so to speak," Melanie explained. "Each is designed for the specific needs of the rider. Our groups consist of five students or less. We try to keep them long enough for the kids to have fun, yet short enough for them not to become too tired—about forty-five minutes."

She gestured toward the arena. "We put the kids through basic walking exercises. Once they're comfortable, we create some fun obstacle courses—nothing too complicated. And as I said, there are two volunteers walking on either side of the horses, so everything is at a slow to moderate pace. We eventually work the children to a skill level that allows them to compete in our own horse shows and play days."

"Really?" Derrick raised his eyebrows as Kara gave him an I-told-you-so look.

Melanie nodded. "And if the weather is bad, we spend time doing ground lessons, which are basically learning about caring for the horses and tack—grooming, feeding and such. We do hands-on demonstrations, plus we show videotapes and let the kids play horse-related computer games. Sometimes we watch videos of the riders themselves, so they can actually see what's needed to improve."

"Wow, I'm impressed," Derrick said. "So, how much do the lessons cost?"

"We don't charge for them." Melanie waved to one of the stable hands as the guy turned a horse out into the arena. "All our funding comes from private donations and local sponsors."

Kara made a mental note to drop a check in the mail.

At the pasture gate, Melanie called to the horses, shaking a bucket of sweet feed to get their attention. "We have a great bunch of horses. They've each been selected based on their disposition. Safety, of course, is a must. We can't have any animal on the place that's spooky or flighty."

"How do you go about training them?" Kara asked.

"It's not all that hard, since we only accept gentle horses that are completely bomb proof. Volunteer trainers, myself included, work with the horses, getting them used to being around wheelchairs, crutches…all that sort of thing. They have to be willing to take a few bumps now and then, when the kids accidentally jostle them."

Melanie caught and haltered a gray gelding and a seal-brown mare. With the help of one of her volunteers—Joy Zane—she demonstrated just how bomb proof the horses were. They weren't afraid of loud noises or sudden movement, though each child was taught—to the best of his or her comprehension—the proper way to pet and talk to the horses.

By the time they'd completed the tour, Kara felt sure Connor would enjoy riding there. If only he'd give the place a chance.

"So," Derrick said, "what do I do to sign Connor up for lessons? If he'll agree to them, that is."

"I'll give you an application to fill out first," Melanie said. "It includes medical and release forms. Once we get them back, we can schedule an evaluation for Connor, which is also free. If he's accepted, we'll chose a time and day for his weekly sessions." Melanie's ready smile creased her face. "You're welcome to bring Connor by to see the place if you'd like. Maybe that will entice him."

After Melanie had given Derrick the application package, he and Kara got back in the truck.

"So, do you think you can talk Connor into coming out here?" Kara asked.

"I don't know." He started the engine, and turned the truck around in the driveway. "I sure hope so. I'll have to make sure it's all right with Shelly, since she'll be the one to sign the forms, but I'm sure she'll okay it. Connor needs something to get him off that danged computer at least once in a while." He glanced at his watch. "Hey, are you hungry?"

Kara looked at her own watch, surprised to see it was already twelve-thirty. "I could stand a bite to eat."

"What are you in the mood for?"

You're in the mood for some loving from a sexy cowboy...one in particular.

"Uh, chicken?" *She was chicken.*

"Sounds like a winner." Derrick drove into town and parked beneath the familiar red-and-white sign.

The sun dipped behind a spread of gray clouds as they entered the restaurant. They gave the cashier their orders, and Derrick refused Kara's attempt to pay. "I've got it."

"Thanks." Kara shifted uncomfortably. The outing was beginning to feel more personal than she'd intended.

"Want to eat outside?" he asked when their order came up.

"Sure."

He held the door for her, pushing it open with one hip, while he balanced their food and drinks on a plastic tray. They sat at one of the umbrella-covered tables between the building and parking lot. Kara bit into a drumstick, suddenly conscious of how messy chicken was. But the flavor erased all other thoughts. She licked her fingers, and Derrick's eyes followed the movement.

"Finger-licking good," he said.

"Mmm-hmm." Kara swallowed her mouthful, her eyes following the movement of his tongue.

What was wrong with her?

Too long alone…too long without Evan. *Too long without sex.*

The chirp of a cell phone made her look at her purse, but Derrick quickly wiped his fingers on a paper napkin. "It's mine." He pulled the phone from a clip on his belt, checking the display. An odd look crossed his face. "Hello?"

He listened, his expression solemn, and Kara wondered if something was wrong.

"That's fine, Mom," Derrick said at last. "We can do that. I won't, don't worry." He turned partially away, voice lowered. "I love you, too. Please don't cry."

Kara had started to get up to throw away her used napkins in the nearby trash can as an excuse to give him some privacy. But he closed the phone and clipped it back on his belt. His face was pinched…drawn.

"Is everything okay?"

"Not really." With a plastic fork, he poked absent-mindedly at his mashed potatoes, swirling the gravy. "As you may have guessed, that was my mom. I haven't seen her—or my dad—in quite a while."

"Didn't you say they live near Miles City?" Kara tried to tamp down her curiosity.

"Yeah, they do. But…it's complicated."

"You don't have to explain." She broke off a piece of her biscuit, just to give her hands something to do. For a minute, Kara thought he wasn't going to reply.

"I don't normally like to talk about it. But damn it, it's eating me up inside." He clenched his fist, his eyes full of hurt and anger.

Impulsively, Kara reached out and touched his arm. "Can I help? I'm a good listener."

Again, he hesitated. "My dad basically hasn't spoken to me since Connor's accident. He blames me for what happened, same as I blame myself."

Kara barely hid her shock. "My God. Derrick, it wasn't your fault. You were a kid."

"I should've known better." The look on his face broke her heart. "Connor is Mom and Dad's only grandchild. I could've killed him. My dad refuses to forgive me for that."

"How can your father be so harsh?" She shook her head. "But your mom…?"

"She hadn't called me in ages until a couple of weeks ago."

Derrick explained about his mother's cancer scare and ensuing hysterectomy. "She wants to put everything behind us, but Dad's against it. He's out getting a haircut right now, which is why she was able to call. Mom wants to find a way to see me without him finding out, but I'm not sure exactly how to do that."

"That's awful—that your dad is hanging onto his anger." Kara chewed her thumbnail, trying to process it. "Is there anything I can do to help?"

Derrick laid down his fork and pushed his plate away. "I doubt anyone will ever be able to reach him."

At that moment, the dark clouds overhead—which Kara hadn't paid attention to—opened up, letting loose a stream of rain. It spattered against the red-and-white umbrella overhead, and a sudden gust of wind caught Kara's plate, sending it sailing into the gutter—coleslaw, drumstick and all. She let out a shriek, hunching her shoulders beneath the onslaught.

Derrick clamped a hand on his own plate in the nick of time. "Talk about the chicken that flew the coop."

Kara laughed. "And it wasn't even a wing."

"Make a run for the truck." Ducking, Derrick chased after her plate and scattered utensils.

Kara jumped into the pickup, and slammed the door shut. Through the rain-blurred windshield, she watched him dump their trash into the nearby plastic barrel, then race for the truck. The rain pounded against the pickup's roof as Derrick slid inside. Water flowed in rivulets from the brim of his hat, and his spattered shirt clung to his chest.

Kara looked hastily away. "Where the heck did that come from?"

"It looks like a doozy." Derrick started the engine and flipped on the windshield wipers, then the radio. "Good thing it waited until after our trip to the riding center."

"Yeah." She buckled her seat belt, and they headed for home.

But the storm quickly swelled into a gulley-washer, and a few short blocks later, a minor fender bender involving three cars brought traffic to a halt at a main intersection.

"Damn!" Derrick peered through the blur of rain. "Looks like we're going to be here for a bit." He turned off the engine, leaving the ignition on so he could play the radio.

Kara became all too aware that they were alone, inside the intimate enclosure of the Chevy's compact cab. With the windshield wipers off, the storm obscured the view, giving the truck's interior a cozy ambiance. To make matters worse, Kara couldn't come up with a single word of small talk. And then a Rascal Flatts song—one of her favorites—came on the radio and Derrick began to sing.

His voice was rich and full. Even without his guitar, he sounded great. It was a love song, poignant and moving. She swallowed hard over the sudden dryness in her throat.

Oh, God.

Derrick wasn't just singing. He was singing to her.

Kara tried not to squirm, but she wanted to leap out of the truck and run. Out of sheer desperation, she began to sing along. Maybe if she pretended they were both just singing with the radio….

Kara belted out the words as the song picked up in volume, her eyes on the rain-washed windshield. She could barely make out the road crew as they worked to clear away the accident.

Derrick's laughter made her head whip around. "What?"

Laugh lines creased the corners of his eyes, and he draped one arm over the steering wheel, staring at her.

"Don't quit your day job, sugar," he said, chuckling.

Mortified, Kara felt her face warm. She'd always thought her shower voice sounded pretty fair. "Are you saying my singing sucks?"

"Not my exact words."

Without thinking, she gave him a playful smack

on the arm, her own laughter bubbling up. "That's not funny!"

Gently, Derrick caught hold of her wrist. His expression went from playful to something far more serious, and he leaned closer as well. Kara's heart pounded so hard, she was sure he could hear it, even over the noise of the storm. He was going to kiss her. And Lord help her, she wanted to let him.

Instead, she pulled abruptly away. She couldn't even look Derrick in the eye—couldn't look at him at all. Her mother-in-law was right. It was too soon. Kara truly didn't care about other people's opinions.

What she did care about was Evan.

CHAPTER EIGHT

DERRICK FELT LIKE A FOOL. What had possessed him to try to kiss Kara? Her obvious discomfort made him wonder if he should apologize or act like nothing had happened.

"Oh, look." Kara pointed. "I think they've got the accident cleaned up."

"Yeah. Looks like it."

Turning off the radio, he started the truck and drove through the intersection. *Kiss her...?* Hell, he shouldn't have even sung to her. Not here. Not in his truck, with the two of them alone. The confidence he'd felt moments before shriveled like a balloon without helium.

Chalk it up to not getting laid since God made dirt.

When his parental rights had been revoked, back when Connor was small, Derrick had gone on a "woman binge." He'd bedded every groupie that came his way. But as time passed, and he gradually earned more of it with his son, women had taken a back seat.

Since the accident, he hadn't been willing to give a woman what he couldn't seem to unlock from himself—his true feelings. Emotions.

He dropped Kara off at her place. "Thanks for going with me."

For the first time since they'd left the intersection, she met his gaze. "You're welcome. I hope Connor will reconsider the riding center."

"We'll see."

She opened the door and got out. "Thanks for the ride. Be careful on your long drive home."

"I'll try not to get any speeding tickets."

He watched her disappear through her front door before he backed out of the driveway.

ON SUNDAY, Derrick took his morning coffee and his guitar out onto the side porch. His next-door neighbors had already left for church. He should be safe playing without disturbing anyone, if he didn't get too loud. While he missed Connor, time alone enabled him to write new songs and practice old ones. He needed time alone to simply lose himself in his music.

The temperature was still pleasantly cool as Derrick propped the Gibson across his lap. The familiarity of the strings beneath his fingers relaxed him better than a shot of whiskey. Softly, he began to strum. He sang a slow, quiet song—one of Buddy Jewell's—about the southland.

A few songs later he was in the middle of a Brad Cotter tune, when he opened his eyes and saw Kara standing on the porch, keys and a cell phone in hand.

"Don't stop," she said, smiling. "I was enjoying it."

Derrick chuckled. "I didn't even hear you walk up."

"You really get into your music. That's a good thing."

"Sometimes." He set the guitar down. "So, what are you doing up so early on a Sunday?"

"I thought I'd go for a ride. It's too nice to stay indoors."

He nodded, uncomfortable at the memory of the previous day. He still felt like a bumbling teenager, trying to kiss the girl.

"Would you like to come?"

"Riding?"

"Yeah. I'm pretty sure I can borrow a horse for you." Kara scuffed the toe of her cowboy boot against the porch, looking down at her feet. "I, uh, feel sort of stupid about how I acted yesterday."

The idea of going on a horseback ride—something he hadn't done in ages—appealed to him. Alone, out on the trail with Kara...

"Sure. But I'm pretty rusty." He grinned, moving to put his guitar away. "I haven't ridden since I was a kid."

"Not that long ago, then."

He laughed. "Let me get my hat. If I'm going to play cowboy, I'd better look the part."

She smiled, and what he saw in her eyes... Kara may still be in love with her husband, but her body language spoke directly to him. He wondered if she was even aware of it.

He put his guitar in the house, grabbed his hat and followed Kara to her pickup. She'd already loaded her tack in the back, and Lady stood on the bench seat, her head poking through the open passenger window.

"Hey, there, Lassie," Derrick said, ruffling the dog's silky coat. "Where's Timmy?"

Lady barked.

"In the well? Shall we get him? Huh?"

The collie barked more furiously, tail wagging, and Kara burst out laughing.

"You're a nut."

He grinned at her, then climbed into the Ford, coaxing Lady over. "She likes to go riding with you, huh?"

"Yep. She's really good about staying close to my horse...except when she decides to take a swim." Kara put on her sunglasses and they were off. "I called the boarding stable on my cell. Ray and Sharon—the people who own the place—have four horses. They said you're welcome to borrow one."

"Sounds good."

When they pulled into the stable yard the place seemed quiet, with only a few cars and trucks parked there. Lady hopped out of the truck, and tagged at Kara's heels as they walked to the barn.

Kara opened a stall door. "This is Indio."

Derrick stared in admiration at the Appaloosa mare. She had enough muscle to show she had quarter horse blood in her lineage, and he ran his hand admiringly over her loudly colored grulla coat. White spots blended into the mousy, gray-brown from neck to barrel, and the mare's white-blanketed rump bore huge, peacock spots of dark brown and black. She stood about fifteen and a half hands—fairly tall.

"Man, now that's a horse," Derrick said.

Kara beamed. "Thank you. I like her."

Obviously an understatement. Kara stroked Indio, and cooed to her as she slipped a purple nylon halter over the mare's head, then led her from the box stall. After tying Indio to the hitching post, Kara motioned for Derrick to follow. In a pasture out back of the barn, she pointed out Ray and Sharon's horses. "Take your pick."

Getting closer, he looked them over, studying their body language, their eyes. The look in a horse's eye told a lot about its disposition. "I think I'll stick with the red roan. He seems steady enough."

"He is." Kara took a halter from where it hung on a fence post, and the roan willingly ducked his head. "This is Boomer, but don't let the name fool you. As you can see, he's a real sweetie. Ray and Sharon's grandkids ride him all the time."

"Sounds right up my alley."

He took pleasure in the simple act of leading the horse back to the hitching post, then brushing him and tacking him up. His fingers moved easily on the cinch, unlocking memories from his childhood. There'd been a time when Derrick had ridden every single day, rain or shine. He wished Connor could know that joy.

Trees arced over the bridle path, offering a pleasant covering of shade as Derrick rode along beside Kara. True to her promise, Boomer handled easily, and soon they were traveling down the trail at a jog.

"Want to lope?" Kara asked.

"Sure." Clucking to Boomer as he squeezed the gelding with his legs, Derrick relaxed in the saddle.

He loved the feel of the leather and the power of the living, breathing animal beneath him. And he loved being with Kara. By the time they slowed to a walk, he felt as if it had been mere hours, not years, since he'd been on the back of a horse. He felt a familiar sense of calm, much the same as when he played his music.

"Looks like you haven't lost your touch," Kara said.

"Guess not. This feels pretty good.... Kara, what made you ask me to go riding today?" The words were out before he could think them through.

Her hazel eyes were serious. "I told you—I wanted to talk to you about yesterday."

"I know, but…that day I helped you carry your tack out to your truck, I got the impression you'd rather I didn't ride with you."

A blush colored her creamy complexion. "You're right."

"So, what made you change your mind? We could've talked on my porch."

"You should've said something." She pulled Indio up short. "We can go back if you'd like. I'm sorry."

"No." He groped for the right words. "I want to ride with you, Kara. I'm just curious what changed your mind—that's all."

She nudged Indio back into a walk. "I owe you an explanation."

"For…?"

"For the way I've been acting. It has nothing to do with you personally."

He remained quiet, listening.

"I've had a really hard time coping with Evan's death." Kara's voice grew thick, and she swallowed hard before continuing. "At times, I still wake up in the morning expecting to find him lying beside me. And then it hits me. He's gone. Forever. It's taken every ounce of strength to get out of bed each day. Keep doing normal, everyday things."

"Is there anything I can do to help?" he asked softly.

She shook her head. "That's just it. Nothing can change what I feel. I've tried riding, working overtime…" She raised her hands, lifting the reins, in a gesture of hopelessness. "Keeping busy helps."

"It takes time," Derrick said. "I know it's not the same thing, but I had nightmares for months after Connor's accident."

Kara looked at him with her pretty eyes, her expression softening. "That's why I pulled away yesterday, Derrick. I'm not ready to move on."

He couldn't help feeling disappointed, even though he'd already sensed it. "I understand."

Still, life was short and unpredictable, and you had to learn to cope. Kara couldn't change what had happened to Evan, but she could choose how or how not to move forward with her life.

"I just wanted you to know it's not you," she reiterated. "You're a nice guy, Derrick. And I enjoy your company. But that's all I can give you right now."

"I really do understand."

"All right…. So, have you talked to Connor since he went back to Shelly's?" Kara asked, clearly relieved to change the topic.

"I spoke to him on the phone yesterday. He was going to see a movie with his friend, Kevin."

"That's nice. Did he mention the riding center?"

"No. And I thought it might be best to wait until he gets home."

"Hopefully he'll give it a shot."

Derrick began to relax. If he couldn't develop a relationship with Kara, he'd settle for what she offered—her company.

He'd be sure to remind himself of that in the night, as he lay in his bed, which was too big for one person.

TWO WEEKS LATER, Derrick picked Connor up and took him out for their usual Friday burgers.

The past Sunday was Father's Day, and even though Connor had still been at Shelly's house, she'd let him spend the day with Derrick. He'd taken Connor to the western store to buy new jeans. The boy seemed to be going through a growth spurt, and it showed in his appetite as well as his clothes. They'd dined on giant, smothered burritos and super nachos, before taking in a movie.

The time apart had seemed to make a difference in Connor's attitude, and things were a little less tense between them.

"So, what all did you do at your mom's?" Derrick asked as he drove Connor home from the burger joint.

Connor shrugged. "Same old stuff. We rented videos, some computer games. Kevin came over a couple of times."

"I went out to God's Little Acre with Kara while you were gone, and it's actually a pretty nice setup. Not what you'd expect, really."

"Yeah?" Connor eyed him warily.

"There are a few kids close to your age in one of the groups."

"How close?"

Derrick shrugged. "Twelve."

Connor let out a snort. "Twelve isn't close, Dad. Twelve is still a baby."

He'd forgotten how much difference two years made to a kid. "I suppose. But I still think you ought to give the place a try."

"Hey, look." Connor pointed as they turned down their street, in an obvious effort to change the subject. "Kara's waxing her truck. Can I go over and see if she needs some help?"

"Sure." Surprised by the boy's generosity, even if it was avoidance, Derrick pulled to a halt at the curb in front of Kara's house. He called a greeting to her, then got Connor's wheelchair out of the camper shell. He watched as his son maneuvered himself from the S-10 into the wheelchair. Connor might not handle his handicap very well emotionally at times, but he'd certainly adapted to it physically.

"Hey, Connor," Kara greeted, walking their way. "What's up?"

"Your truck is so awesome," he said. "Can I help you wax it?"

She grinned. "Be my guest. It's not exactly my favorite job in the world."

"Then why do you do it?"

Kara met Derrick's gaze, her smile slipping. "Well…the Ford was Evan's pride and joy. He had it custom painted, and he always waxed it every couple of weeks. I feel…obligated to do the same."

Connor nodded, not noticing Kara's discomfort.

"You sure you don't mind Connor hanging out?" Derrick asked, doing his best to ignore the reminder that he was competing with a dead guy.

"Not at all."

"See you later, then." He climbed back into the Chevy, and drove across the street.

He parked, then walked inside the house without a backward glance.

He had a feeling Evan's spirit was up on him by several points.

KARA IGNORED the shaky feeling that stayed with her even after Derrick disappeared from view. That he didn't seem to like it when she brought up Evan's name was becoming more and more obvious. Maybe Liz was right. Maybe she should stay away from Derrick.

But then, it really shouldn't matter. She was only his neighbor…just a woman he spent time with on occasion.

A woman who was falling for him, like it or not.

"So, how was your visit with your mom?" she asked.

"Fine." Connor worked at rubbing wax onto the Chevy's glossy black paint. "I played my guitar a lot."

"You did?" She still didn't understand why Connor wanted to hide his talents from his dad.

"I think I might've written a pretty good song, too. Well, part of one anyway. It's not finished yet."

"Good for you." Kara buffed dried wax from the truck's hood. "Connor, why don't you want your dad to know about your music?"

His expression grew somber. "I just don't, that's all."

"You must have a reason," she said mildly. "Sure you don't want to talk about it?"

He sighed, a very adultlike sound. And suddenly Kara was aware of how quickly the fourteen-year-old must have had to face adult issues in dealing with his handicap and the lifelong aftermath of the wreck Derrick had caused.

"I could never be like him."

"What do you mean?"

"You know. The way he has all those women drooling over him when he's up on stage." Connor rubbed the round sponge against the can of wax, getting more on his hand than on the sponge.

Duh, Kara. Connor was afraid of being made fun of. Of not being attractive to girls his own age.

"You're a talented singer *and* guitar player," she said. "You don't have to be like your dad. You only have to be yourself."

Vigorously, he worked the sponge over the truck's front fender.

Kara was sorry she'd spoiled their light mood. "So, you really like this pickup, huh?"

"Sure."

"Guess so, or you wouldn't be helping me wax it." She quirked her mouth. "Say, how would you like to go for a ride in it? That is, if your dad won't mind."

"Really?" he asked eagerly.

"Sure. I might even let you drive."

"Get out of here."

"No, seriously. There's an alfalfa field on the ranch where I board my horse, and Ray and Sharon take their grandkids out there sometimes and let them drive when they're baling hay. The ground has a slight downward slope. We'll just put the truck in Drive, I'll sit beside you, and you can steer. We'll be crawling along—nothing dangerous. If we need to stop, I'll hit the brake."

Connor grinned. "Sweet!" But then just as quickly he sobered. "I doubt my dad will go for it."

"Then we won't tell him." Kara knew she was overstepping her boundaries, and that she had no right. But Connor seemed to need something to boost his confidence. To get him out from the protective blanket Derrick had draped around him. After all, he was just four years away from being an adult. And besides, she had an idea.

Connor licked his bottom lip. "You mean it?"

"Sure." Kara wiped the last of the wax from the Ford's hood, then cleaned her hands on a rag. "Hey, I remember what it's like to be fourteen. You don't think I told my parents everything I did, do you?"

He laughed.

"So, why don't you come in and we'll wash up. Then we'll call your dad and see if he'll let me take you for a spin."

"Cool!"

In the house, Kara looked up Derrick's number in the half-inch-thick phone book for Sage Bend and its surrounding towns.

"What's up, Connor?" Derrick answered.

"You should believe your caller ID," Kara said. "It's me." She lowered her voice. "Derrick, Connor wants to go for a ride in my truck. I thought I might take him to see Indio, if that's all right with you. Maybe that will inspire him to ride."

"Yeah, sure. No problem."

"Okay. We won't be long." She hung up just as Connor came into the living room.

"Was that Dad?"

"Yep. And we're all set. He said you can go."

"Sweet!" Connor headed for the door, and Kara helped guide him over the threshold and down the steps.

"I see your dad has been working on a wheelchair

ramp for you," she said as they headed for the Ford. "That'll make things easier, huh?"

"Yeah. I hate stairs." Connor swung deftly into the pickup with scarcely any help from her, even though the truck sat higher off the ground than Derrick's S-10. The strength in the boy's arms surprised Kara.

She thought back to the night at the Silver Spur, when he'd tipped over, but managed to catch his balance on one arm. The kid was wiry all right. And what he lacked for in physical ability, he seemed to more than make up for in spirit.

Even if he didn't seem to recognize it.

CHAPTER NINE

DERRICK KNEW THE THOUGHT was ridiculous, but for just a heartbeat as he'd hung up the phone, he'd second-guessed letting Connor go driving with Kara.

Stupid.

The first time Derrick had driven with Connor in the car after the accident was something he'd never forget. He'd nearly suffered a full-blown panic attack. Scared to death that if he so much as dented a fender while parking, Shelly would make sure he never saw Connor again.

The first time he'd been allowed to take his son for the entire day, Derrick had been so happy, he'd wanted to go someplace special.

They never made it to the zoo in Billings. The sight of Connor in his booster seat in the rearview mirror...déjà vu. Derrick had lost his nerve.

Now Derrick sat on the front porch, staring at Kara's empty driveway. *He's fine. They're fine...everything is fine.*

The ringing phone startled him, and he hurried to answer.

"Hello?"

"Derrick, it's Mom." She hesitated. "How are you?"

He let out his breath and sank onto the couch. "I'm fine, Mom. Are you all right? Are you feeling okay?"

"Actually, I'm doing much better. I…uh…I'm here in town. In Sage Bend. I was wondering…is it all right if I come over?"

"Of course." He couldn't believe she was here.

"Are you sure? I don't want to put you on the spot."

"Yes." The word came out hasty, panicked. Derrick softened his tone. "I'd love to see you, Mom. Did Connor tell you we moved?"

"He did. I know right where your house is."

"Okay. I'll see you in a few minutes, then."

He hung up the phone, caught up in a strange mixture of emotions. He had butterflies in his stomach—no, bats. Restless, Derrick went back outside and paced the length of the porch. It wasn't more than five minutes before he saw a white Buick turn to park in front of his house.

He didn't know whether to laugh or cry when his mother got out of the car. He'd seen her, maybe twice, in the last twelve years, and he wasn't sure he would've recognized her if they'd passed on the street.

Derrick hurried down the steps, his long strides eating up the distance between them.

"Mom. It's…good to see you." He swallowed over the sudden lump in his throat. "Really good."

"Oh, Derrick." She reached for him, tears spilling down her cheeks, washing makeup away from lines he didn't remember. Her hair had gone completely gray, and she'd never weighed so little, but she was here. Alive and well.

He hugged her, taking in her familiar scent of perfume and powder, memories washing over him.

His mother, laughing as she pitched a baseball to him when he was nine. The two of them, taking a drive together when he'd gotten his learner's permit. Carolyn beaming down at her newborn grandson, as she held Connor.

Derrick didn't want to recall the bad times… when she'd taken his father's side and turned her back on him. He'd been only twenty.

She could've died if the ovarian tumors had been cancerous. What if he'd never seen her again?

He drew back, still holding on to her, staring into her blue eyes. "Mom, are you sure you're feeling all right? Should you be driving this far so soon?" It had been—what? Five weeks—six—since she'd phoned him?

"So soon?" Carolyn laughed through her tears. "It doesn't feel soon enough to me, son." She hugged him tight again. "I can't believe I'm finally standing here."

"Neither can I." Derrick sniffed, wiping his

cheeks with the back of his hand. "Come in and sit down. Let me get you something cold to drink."

"I'd love that." Carolyn climbed the steps, looking at the house as she went. The tension he'd initially seen on her face vanished, and she appeared more like her old self. "This is a lovely little house. I remember when it was painted pale blue, and the Rogers family lived here. They had four girls, a few years younger than you."

"I don't remember," Derrick said, holding the screen door for her. "Make yourself comfortable." He wished he could follow his own advice. But he still had butterflies. "What would you like to drink? I've got pop, water or ice tea."

"I'm fine, Derrick, really." She sat on the couch, still clinging to his hand. "Seeing you is all I need."

He sat beside her, and she touched his cheek. "I can't believe how much you've changed. My God, you're a grown man!" She put one hand over her mouth, tears squeezing from her eyes again. "You're a grown man, and I don't even know you...my own son. How could I have been so stupid?"

"Hey, Mom. Shhh." Derrick held her while she cried it out, his chest tight. After her tears subsided, he got her some tissues and a glass of water in spite of her protests.

"I'm sorry, Derrick. I didn't mean to fall to pieces on you like that."

"Don't worry about it." He clasped his hands in his lap, not knowing where to begin…what to say.

"I've missed you so much," Carolyn said, blowing her nose.

"I missed you, too." More than he'd ever realized.

At first, he'd felt only hurt and anger when his parents had pushed him away. He couldn't begin to imagine doing the same thing to Connor. But his resentment had faded with the passage of time.

"How did you get here without Dad throwing a fit?"

Carolyn laughed without humor. "It wasn't easy. I had to wait until he wasn't home. I left him a note, which he should've gotten by now. I haven't checked my cell phone messages, but I'm sure your father will be furious."

"I don't want to cause trouble between the two of you."

"You're not." She took his hand. "Besides, I don't care if the old coot is mad. I'm sick of letting him push me around." Her voice carried a strength Derrick didn't remember her having. "I guess the cancer scare gave me some backbone. This craziness has gone on long enough. You're my only son—my only child. And I'm tired of not having you in my life. If your father doesn't like that…well, he'll just have to learn to live with it." She took another sip of water, then clenched the glass in both hands. Her fingers looked somewhat aged, but strong.

They sat in silence a moment. "Is Connor here?" Carolyn finally asked.

"No. He's…with a friend."

She nodded. "That's just as well." She looked both uncertain and determined. "I think it's time you know why your father was so harsh in judging you after the accident."

Derrick frowned. "What do you mean? I already know why. Because of what I did to Connor."

"Yes, but there's more to it than that. There's a reason why Vernon reacted the way he did. A reason that has nothing to do with you at all."

KARA TOOK THE LONG WAY to the stable so she could drive past God's Little Acre. No harm in pointing it out. As she and Connor neared it, she slowed the Ford considerably. Ahead, she spotted a young girl on a flashy black-and-white Paint horse headed their way, riding on the shoulder of the road.

"Wow, that's some horse," Kara said.

"Yeah."

But she could see the horse wasn't the only thing that had caught Connor's attention.

The girl on the Paint looked to be close to Connor's age, and she was cute. Her dark brown hair hung all the way to her waist, tied in a neat ponytail beneath her riding helmet. She stared back at Connor, lifting her hand as they passed.

Connor turned to look over his shoulder through the pickup's back window, and Kara hid a smile. "I love a purple horse," she said.

"Yeah," Connor repeated. Then he looked at her and frowned. "Huh?"

Kara laughed. "Nothing. I'm just razzing you." She pointed as they neared the driveway of Melanie Spencer's ranch. "That's the riding center I told you about. Have you been by here before?"

"Is that why you drove me out here? To try to get me to change my mind about riding with a bunch of retards?"

Damn! "No, it's not." Kara gave him a look of reprimand. "I may not be your mom, but I won't tolerate that kind of talk. How would you feel if someone called you a cripple instead of handicapped, or physically challenged?"

"They *have*," Connor said with a huff. "They're just stupid words, that's all. Dressing them up doesn't change what I am or what those kids at God's Little Acre are."

"No, it doesn't," Kara said. "But it's still rude."

He glanced defiantly at her. "Fine. Sorry."

"Connor, why do you do that?"

"Do what?"

"Put yourself down that way. My God, you're a smart, talented young man. And you're fun to be with, well, most of the time anyway." She softened the words with a smile. "You need to believe in yourself."

He shrugged. "Whatever."

"And would it be so horrible to do something nice for your dad?"

"What do you mean?"

"He'd really like you to give the riding center a try. It's good to get out and get fresh air and exercise, and you might even have fun."

"I get fresh air sitting on the porch, and I can't exercise."

"That's not true." Kara turned one hand palm up. "Look how strong and muscular your arms are. You must work your upper body during physical therapy, right?"

"I guess so." Connor shrugged.

"Your dad loves you just the way you are, Connor. He only wants what's best for you."

His face reddened. "I know that. But I'm not so sure he doesn't wish he had a son who could run and toss the old football with him. Or rope a calf."

"Why can't you rope a calf?"

"You're joking, right?"

"Are your arms paralyzed?"

"No."

"Do you rope with your feet?"

He let out a laugh. "Guess not."

"Well, there you go." Kara pursed her lips.

"You've got great upper body strength, and there's no reason why you can't ride a horse."

The look on Connor's face changed, just enough for her to see he was thinking. "Maybe you won't break any calf-roping records," Kara continued, "but you can still have a good time." She drove on, leaving God's Little Acre behind. "You'll see when you meet Indio."

"I don't know." Connor stared out the windshield.

"Well, I do. And don't forget about our drive."

He brightened. "Now you're talkin'."

Kara laughed and cranked up the radio. Connor grinned, then sang along with Hank Williams.

DERRICK STARED at his mother. "I'm listening," he said. "What do you mean, it didn't have anything to do with me?"

Carolyn leaned back against the couch. "Your father had a younger brother, your Uncle Rex."

Derrick nodded. "The one he'd never talk about. He died young."

"Very young." Her eyes took on a faraway look. "Your father was five years older than Rex. When Vernon was thirteen, he took Rex pheasant hunting. Your grandpa had told him not to go—not without adult supervision—but your father didn't listen."

Derek could guess where this story was going.

"Vernon knew enough not to climb through a

fence with a loaded shotgun. So he leaned his 12 gauge against a fence post."

She closed her eyes briefly.

"Rex got shot," Derrick said quietly.

"Yes. It was so horrible. When Rex pressed down on the barbed wire and climbed through, the shotgun fell over and went off. The shot hit him in the face and the chest. He was gone before Vernon could get back with help."

"My God."

"Vernon told me he'd never forget the sight of Rex lying on the ground, so still and…blood everywhere. Or the wail your grandpa let out when he saw his baby boy lying there like that. Your grandparents didn't blame Vernon, but your father never forgave himself. He never so much as touched a gun again, and from what your grandma told me, Vernon was never the same person after that."

"I guess not." Derrick swallowed hard, fully understanding the scope of his dad's guilt.

"So when you wrecked your car and Connor got hurt…"

Derrick felt sick.

Carolyn swiped away tears. "In your father's eyes, his brother had died because he acted irresponsibly in taking him hunting when he'd been told not to. And you acted just as irresponsibly in drag racing with Connor in the car."

Derrick laid a shaky hand on her shoulder. He was…angry, sad…guilty. "I *was* careless, and what I did was plain stupid."

"But you were just a kid." Carolyn slipped her hand over his. "Like Vernon was."

Derrick laughed without humor. "Looks like dad and I have something in common after all."

Carolyn's eyes filled with sadness. "They were both terrible accidents. And I can't get your father to see the hypocrisy in what we've done to you."

"You didn't do anything to me," Derrick said quietly. "I brought it on myself."

"You made a mistake," Carolyn said, squeezing his hand for emphasis. "I finally see that—and I can forgive you, son. Vernon needs to forgive you so he can move on." She started to cry again. "I'm just sorry it took me so long to realize this."

"Don't cry, Mom." Derrick took a tissue and wiped the tears from her cheeks. "I love you. I'm so glad you came to see me. Told me about Rex."

"I should've told you sooner. You have to get past the guilt, Derrick."

"How can I? I ruined Connor's life."

"No!" The single word held so much pain. "His life isn't ruined, just because he's handicapped. Derrick, why can't you see that? I've forgiven you for what you did, and now you need to forgive yourself." She stood and paced. "Damn it, you're every bit as stubborn as your father!"

Derrick shrugged. "Looks like."

CHAPTER TEN

CONNOR SAT BUCKLED into the driver's seat beside Kara. To their left, the hayfield, to their right, a wire fence.

"Here we go."

"What if I hit the fence?" Connor ran his hands nervously around the steering wheel, then pointed at the field. "Can't we drive out there?"

"Uh-uh. Sharon said we could drive around the perimeter, but if I ruin her alfalfa, she'll strangle me." Kara smiled. "Come on. You can do it. I'm right here and, like I said, I'll step on the brake if you need me to. Here." She slid her left foot over and pressed the brake, bumping Connor's knee even though she'd tucked his legs as far to the left as she could. "Sorry."

"It's okay. I can't feel it." He grinned crookedly.

Kara chuckled. "All right, then." She gestured toward the gearshift on the steering column. "Put 'er in Drive."

Hesitantly, Connor took hold of the gearshift and

maneuvered it until he had the red-orange indicator lined up on *D*.

"Ready?" Kara asked.

He nodded, and she took her foot off the brake and pulled her leg out of his way. The Ford rolled slowly forward, moving at a snail's pace.

Connor's eyes lit up. "Rad!"

Kara laughed.

On the slight slope of the hayfield, the truck continued to roll. Connor focused intently, the tip of his tongue poking between his lips as he steered.

"Can we go faster?" he asked.

"All right, but only a little." She slid her foot onto the accelerator, then laughed as she pressed too hard and the truck jerked forward. "Sorry. It's awkward, using my left foot."

"No problem." Connor gripped the wheel. "I've got it."

They rolled along, Kara pressing the pedal just enough to keep the Ford moving. "You've got a baler coming up," she said unnecessarily. The piece of farm machinery sat parked on the edge of the field, just inside the fence.

"Duh," Connor said. But he smiled.

Intent on the baler, Kara didn't notice a dip in the field until the Ford rolled into it. The dip was just deep enough to keep the pickup from continuing under its own momentum.

"Crap," Connor said. "We're stuck."

"Naw. We got hung up a bit, that's all." Kara moved to press down on the accelerator again, but a sudden cramp in her thigh caused her leg to spasm. Her foot slipped, and she hit the gas.

The truck lurched forward, straight into the baler chute. The forklike apparatus punctured the pickup's radiator, and the pungent smell of antifreeze drifted into the air as Kara finally found the brake.

"Put it in Park!" Kara said.

Eyes wide, Connor fumbled with the gearshift, and managed to do as she said. Kara turned off the key, killing the engine. The silence was broken only by the radiator's hissing. Kara and Connor exchanged glances, then burst into hysterical laughter.

"Damn—dang, Kara, I'm really sorry."

"I'm the one who stomped on the gas."

"Man, my dad's gonna kill me." He clapped one hand to his forehead.

Kara slid across the seat to the passenger side, then got out to assess the damage. A fist-sized hole in the truck's radiator gaped like a wound where the chute had gone through the grill.

Evan would have been livid.

Kara bit her lip as tears slid down her cheeks. What had she done? She'd ruined the grill...put a dent in the bumper. Not to mention she'd let Connor drive—a decision that wasn't hers to make.

"Kara?" Connor called through the open driver's window. "Aw, man, don't cry. I'm really, really sorry."

Kara wiped her cheeks. Sniffing, she forced a smile. "I told you, it wasn't your fault." She walked around to his side of the truck. "I'm the one who's sorry." She shook her head. "It's me your dad's going to kill."

DERRICK GRABBED THE KEYS to his pickup, unable to wait for Kara to come back. He was eager to see his son and his mother together, with him, for the first time in years.

"Come on, Mom," Derrick said. "We'll drive out to Kara's stable. You can meet her, then we'll all go grab a Coke."

"That sounds lovely, son." Carolyn reached out to stroke his hair. "You don't know how much better I feel, getting everything out in the open."

"Me, too."

When they reached the boarding stable, Derrick frowned. "That's odd. Kara's truck's not here."

"Maybe they already left," Carolyn said.

Derrick shook his head. "We would've passed them on the way out." Unless Kara had driven to God's Little Acre. "I think I know where they might be."

Derrick made a three-point turn in front of the barn, then headed out onto the road.

But as he passed a hayfield, he spotted Kara's pickup, nosed up against a baler. *What the…?*

"That's Kara's truck." Derrick slowed the S-10, checked his mirrors and backed up. The gate to the hayfield stood open, so he drove through.

And just about swallowed his teeth when he saw Connor sitting behind the wheel of Kara's Ford.

Derrick let out an expletive that made Carolyn cringe. "Sorry, Mom. But what the hell is Kara doing?" He wrenched the door of his own truck open, and practically flew out.

"Derrick." Kara looked as guilty as a kid caught shoplifting. "Let me explain. I—"

"Explain?" He gestured angrily toward the Ford. "You let Conner *drive?* Kara, what the hell were you thinking?"

Her gaze darted over his shoulder to Carolyn, then back. "We just wanted to do something fun." Kara lowered her voice. "Something to help boost his confidence."

Derrick let out a bitter laugh. "And crashing your truck into a baler is going to accomplish that, how?"

"Derrick, I'm sorry. Things didn't turn out quite like I'd planned."

"That's just it, Kara! Things never turn out the way we plan. Which is why I—"

"It's not her fault, so don't yell at her!" Connor craned his neck through the window. "Somebody get me out of here."

Derrick got the wheelchair out of the pickup bed,

then held it steady while his son maneuvered into it. Belatedly, the boy noticed Carolyn, standing a few feet away.

"Grandma. What are you doing here?" Connor stared at Derrick, the implications of his grandmother's presence finally registering.

Carolyn smiled. "I decided it was high time I came to see my son." She placed her hand on Derrick's shoulder, then bent and brushed a kiss against Connor's forehead. "How's my favorite grandson?"

"I'm your only grandson." But the teen couldn't quite manage a smile.

Carolyn held her hand out to Kara. "I'm Derrick's mother, Carolyn Mertz."

"Nice to meet you. I'm Kara Tillman." She shook Carolyn's hand, raising her eyes to Derrick.

But he was too mad for niceties. He glared at her, then Connor. "Do one of you want to tell me how this happened?"

"It was my fault—"

"Don't blame Kara—"

The words came out simultaneously, and Kara and Connor looked at each other as though they shared an inside joke.

"You think this is funny?" Derrick placed his hands on his hips.

"I'm sorry." Kara bit her lip. "It's not funny, it's just that…" She laced her fingers together. "I know I acted irresponsibly, Derrick. I had no right to take your son driving, and I apologize. It won't happen again."

"Damned right it won't." It would be a cold day in hell before he trusted her with Connor again.

"Derrick," Carolyn said, "give Kara a chance to explain." She took hold of Connor's wheelchair. "Come on. Let's you and me go on back to the truck." She looked at Derrick. "I can drive him home, if you'd like, then come back for you and Kara in my car."

"That's fine," Derrick said, "since it looks like her pickup isn't going anywhere anytime soon."

Kara scowled at him. "I don't need a ride, thank you, Mrs. Mertz. I'll call a tow truck and arrange for a friend to come get me."

"Whatever you want to do." Carolyn pushed the wheelchair, barely able to move it across the rough surface of the hayfield.

"Let me help you," Derrick said. "I'll be back."

Connor gave him a dark look, then craned his neck around to mouth "bye" to Kara. Carolyn walked beside his chair.

"So, what are you doing here, Grandma? I thought you and Dad..."

"I'll explain on the way back to your place," she said, laying her hand on Connor's shoulder.

Once the teen was settled in the Chevy, Derrick walked around to the driver's door. "Thanks, Mom."

He leaned in through the window to kiss her cheek. "For everything."

"No problem. See you in a bit." She drove away.

Kara was on her cell phone when Derrick returned, talking to someone at the local garage about sending a tow truck. She flipped the phone shut and slipped it into her pocket.

For a moment, they stared at each other. Then Kara pulled the truck's tailgate open and sat on the edge of it. "Have a seat."

Derrick didn't want to sit. He wanted to shake her until her teeth rattled. He pressed both hands against the crown of his cowboy hat in frustration.

"Kara, exactly what the hell happened here?"

She sighed. "I told you. I wanted to do something for Connor to help boost his confidence. He suffers from low self-esteem—did you know that?"

"Of course I know that. I'm his father, aren't I?"

"I know you're his father," Kara said, "and I also know that I had no right to let him drive—"

"Damned right, you didn't! He could've been hurt—*you* could've gotten hurt."

"But," she went on, glaring at him, "I had another reason for doing it, if you'll let me explain."

Derrick folded his arms, standing with feet his spread apart. "I'm all ears."

"Before coming out here, we drove past God's Little Acre...."

Derrick listened as she told him about the conversation she'd had with Connor, and how his interest seemed to peak when she'd mentioned calf-roping.

"I thought it might help encourage him to learn to ride—at Melanie's."

"Kara, get real. Connor may be able to ride, but he won't be able to calf-rope."

"Why not? Who says he has to go fast? And who says he has to use a real calf? A roping dummy can be a lot of fun."

Derrick was momentarily at a loss for words. "I'm sorry, I still don't see the relevance of letting Connor drive."

"Because." She held her hands out, fingers spread. "I figured if Connor saw he could actually do something he'd never thought possible—like drive—then surely he'd realize he can ride a horse!"

Derrick's anger disappeared. Almost.

"I thought it would be perfectly safe for him to steer my truck around the hayfield."

"But you forgot Connor can't work the brake."

"No." She sighed impatiently. "I'm strawberry-blond, Derrick, not blond. I was sitting next to him, so I could brake for him."

"Oh, then that makes it perfectly fine!"

"I wouldn't have tried it anyplace dangerous."

"Connor wrecked your truck."

"Connor didn't wreck it—I did. I hit the gas

instead of the brake." She folded her own arms, mirroring him. "So if you're going to be mad at someone, be mad at me. It wasn't Connor's fault, or his idea, either."

Derrick expelled his breath on a long sigh. Kara's expression was a combination of defiance and contrition.

He wanted to shake her *and* kiss her.

"What am I going to do with you?" Derrick sat on the tailgate beside her.

"I *am* sorry, Derrick," Kara repeated. "You trusted me with your son, and I—"

"Shh." He touched a finger to her lips. "I still trust you, Kara." He brushed his knuckles against her cheek.

"You're not mad?"

"I didn't say that."

She gave him a half smile. "So yell at me already and get it over with."

"I don't want to yell at you." He inched closer. "I want to kiss you."

"Derrick." She pushed away, as though he'd lost his mind. But something else was in her expression, something that made him lean toward her.

"Don't talk," Derrick said. "Just kiss me." He cradled her face in his hands.

She tensed. "I can't."

"Yes, you can." He brushed his lips across hers. Softly. Slowly.

"Derrick…"

He kissed away her protests, and hesitantly, she finally kissed him back. He laced his hands through her hair and slipped his tongue between her lips. Kara moaned, still rigid in his arms. But as he continued to kiss her, she began to relax. Eyes closed, she stroked her tongue against his. Derrick shut his own eyes and lost himself in the moment. For the span of several seconds, there was nothing but the way Kara tasted and felt beneath his touch. Then he felt moisture between their cheeks, and he pulled back to see tears on her face.

"Kara?"

She pressed her knuckles against her mouth. "Derrick, Evan hasn't even been gone a year yet." Her eyes conveyed her confusion and sorrow. "I really…like you, but…I just can't—"

"It's okay, Kara. You don't have to explain." He got up from the tailgate. "I understand."

He was competing with a ghost. A fight he damned well didn't know how to win.

Kara brushed the tears from her eyes. "It's too soon, Derrick. That's all."

He nodded and slipped his hands into his back pockets to keep from reaching for her again.

"Here comes the tow truck." Kara stood, and flagged the driver down.

Derrick kicked a clod of dirt with the toe of his boot, sending it sailing.

In the span of one evening, he'd gained a mother, lost ground with his son and screwed things up with Kara.

He should've waited, and let her come to him when she was ready.

KARA RODE HOME in Danita's car, only half listening to what her friend was saying. She was too busy reliving the kisses she'd shared with Derrick. They'd felt wrong, yet so right. She had to get ahold of herself. Maybe she would call Liz this week, and invite her to lunch or supper.

"I can't believe you let Connor drive," Danita said for the umpteenth time. "Kara, you're lucky the man doesn't sue you!"

"Sue me? I'm the one with the busted radiator." She'd wrecked Evan's truck, then sat on the tailgate and kissed another man.

"Yes, but you're also the one who put Derrick's son at risk." Danita spoke in her motherly voice. "That was really stupid, *mi hija*."

"It seemed like a good idea at the time."

Danita rolled her eyes. "Boy, have I had my share of those moments."

"Do you think Derrick will invite me to hear his band play tonight?" Kara deepened her voice. "'This next song is dedicated to the brain-dead woman, who let my handicapped son drive her truck. It's called 'Pull Your Head Out of Your Butt, Little Darlin'.'"

Danita laughed. "Okay, we've beat you up enough. You made a mistake, but your intentions were good."

"You know what they say about the road to hell."

"Speaking of hell," Danita said, "I gave Phillip some yesterday."

"Really? What happened?"

"I hired Mathew Drake as my attorney, and he put a restraining order on Phillip after that last phone call. The dumb ass left a message on my answering machine telling me he'd see me dead before he'd see me living in a house *he'd* paid for. How do you like that?"

Kara snorted. "As if you haven't worked your butt off building your cleaning business. You've put more than your share into that house."

"Tell me about it. And all that time, he was off with that slut, and God knows who else. The son of a bitch."

"I'm telling you, success is the sweetest form of revenge," Kara said. "You keep growing your client list, and you'll soon have assistants working *for* you, not with you. Then you'll fall in love with some good-looking guy—possibly a fireman whose name we won't mention—and Phillip will eventually get bored with his bimbo, and realize he gave up the best thing in his life when he lost you. Plus, I hear Mathew Drake is a pitbull in the courtroom."

"He is." Danita grinned slyly. "By the time he's done with Phillip, he'll wish he'd never crossed me."

They pulled up in front of Kara's house. Derrick's truck was there, but Kara saw no sign of a car that might belong to Carolyn Mertz. "Thanks for the ride," she said to Danita.

"No problem, *mi hija.* Call me. I can give you a lift to work on Monday."

Inside the living room, Kara welcomed Lady's enthusiastic greeting, then took her to the backyard. She sat in a lawn chair while Lady trotted purposefully across the grass, nose to the ground. The collie crouched, shifting one hind leg slightly, and cast a very humanlike stare over her shoulder. *Don't look at me. I'm peeing.*

Kara laughed, glad of the small distraction from reliving what had happened between her and Derrick.

She was glad his mother hadn't caught them kissing, or Danita, who'd arrived shortly after the tow truck driver. She was curious, though, what Derrick's mom was doing here. Kara hoped everything was all right.

Maybe Carolyn Mertz's presence meant things were changing. If Derrick could make peace with his mom and dad, he might get past Connor's accident. It might help him move forward, which in turn should help Connor. Lord knew her own good intentions hadn't helped much. Danita was right, she was lucky Derrick hadn't been more upset with her.

A car's engine, slowing as it passed her house, jarred Kara from her thoughts. A neighbor coming home? Or Derrick? Unable to resist, she went to look over the fence. In the fading, evening light, she saw a white Buick park in Derrick's driveway next to his pickup. Carolyn got out of the driver's side, while Derrick went around to the trunk for Connor's wheelchair. He glanced her way, and Kara quickly ducked back out of sight.

Had he seen her? Would he think she was being nosy, spying on him?

Well, wasn't she?

Kara hurried back around the house. Lady eyed her, curious. "Ready to go in? Come on, girl." Kara patted her thigh, and the dog followed.

She'd go to bed early. Curl up with a good book.

And bring an end to this crazy day.

But the phone rang not long after and Kara answered without bothering to check the caller ID.

"Hello?"

For a moment, no one spoke.

"Kara, it's Derrick. I heard what you said earlier about not being ready to move on. But I can't quit thinking about you."

Ditto.

She groped for neutral ground. "Is everything okay? Connor's all right?"

"Yeah, he's fine. My mom is staying over the weekend."

"That's nice."

"My dad didn't think so."

"Oh?"

"It's a long story. Anyway, Mom's a little stressed, and I thought it might do her some good to get out for a while. My band's playing at the Spur tonight, and Mom hasn't heard me pick a guitar in years."

Was he trying to ask her to join them?

"Connor doesn't feel like going with us, and the only time I leave him alone is when I go to work. Connor's too old to need a babysitter, but…"

Kara hid her disappointment. He was calling her because of Connor.

"Kara, I overreacted today. You know how I am with Connor, and, well, I'm trying to learn to cut him slack, but it's hard."

"Derrick, just say whatever it is you're trying to say. Do you want me to keep an eye on him?"

"Would you mind? I don't mean come over here or anything. He'd kill me for that." Wryly, Derrick chuckled. "But none of our other neighbors are home tonight, and I don't like going out and leaving him with no one to contact in case of an emergency, especially since I'll be getting home late. I can't call

Shelly, because I'd prefer she didn't find out what happened today."

Kara could've kicked herself. No matter what he said, he was obviously still tense over the driving incident. Yet he wanted Kara to keep an eye on Connor, in spite of her being the one responsible. She felt like a piece of taffy, being pulled first one way, then the other.

"So, you don't want him to phone his mom if he needs something? You'd rather he phoned me?"

"Yeah, that's about the size of it." Derrick let his breath out on a sigh. "So, that's fine with you?"

"Sure, Derrick."

"Great. Thanks, Kara. I owe you one." He said goodbye and hung up.

Kara stared at the phone before finally putting it back on the charger.

A short time later, she climbed in bed with a paperback romance in hand. She'd forgone her nightgown in exchange for a clean T-shirt over her bra and panties. Her jeans and boots were beside the bed, handy if she needed them, should Connor call.

She fell asleep an hour later with the book in her hands, her thoughts still on Derrick.

CHAPTER ELEVEN

CONNOR LOOKED OUT his window. He could only see
one light on at Kara's. He'd heard his father on the
phone with her earlier, asking Kara to keep an eye
on him. Connor shook his head, disgusted. He never
should've driven her truck. Now his dad was more
determined than ever to treat him like a baby.

At his computer, he signed in to the Billings chat
room as MTcwby89. CanChaser1 was online.

Hey, CC. How's it going?

Hey, MT. Not bad.

What's a pretty girl like u doing home on a Fri. night?

She typed in a blushing smiley face emoticon,
then a wink. Wouldn't u like to know? I could ask
u the same thing.

I'm not a pretty girl. Connor typed back with an
LOL.

No, but you're hot.

So R U.

Kerri didn't respond right away. Connor waited.

Wanna meet me? she typed.

His hands froze on the keyboard. Hell.

Maybe, he stalled. When? Where?

What was he doing? He couldn't meet her.

Do you know the Silver Spur? she typed. In Sage Bend?

Connor's palms turned damp and clammy, and he thought he might drop dead right there. His dad would come home and find him slumped in his wheelchair, the youngest guy to ever die of heart failure.

Not really, he replied. Never been out that way.

U can't miss it. Outside Sage Bend—about 80 miles from Billings.

Connor's mind went blank.

U said U R new in town, Kerri continued. Y not meet me and my friends? Tomorrow is family night at the Spur. Anyone can get in—U don't have to be 21.

Really?

Yup.

What now? His dad's band was playing again tomorrow night, and he'd likely have to go, especially with Grandma Mertz visiting.

His fingers flew across the keyboard. That's cool, but I already have plans. Sorry.

Hey, no problem. They'll have it again next week—first Sat. of the month. So how 'bout it, cowboy? Another smiley emoticon.

Connor keyed a grin. Sure. Why not. He could always make up something later…some reason why MTcwby89 hadn't shown.

Sweet, Kerri replied. I'll take your picture with me, so I can be sure to find you.

That'll work. I'll take yours 2.

It's a date. Gotta go. Bye 4 now.

"Yeah, goodbye." Connor spoke out loud, glaring at his laptop monitor. That fake picture. "Great. Just great."

A familiar name flashed onto the screen as SoccorMan1 signed in to the chat room. Kevin.

Whaz up? You online ConMan1?

Right here. R U blind or just stupid? He loved razzing Kevin, teasing him about being an airhead jock.

His friend always gave back as good as he got. Fingers on the keyboard, Connor waited for a response, ready to fire another in return.

Huh? Who R U, MTcwby?

All the blood rushed from Connor's head. Quickly, he logged off as MTcwby89, then logged back on as ConMan1.

Damn, talk about being dumb!

Yeah, I'm online. Let's go to IM.

OK.

Kevin's screen name showed he'd logged off.

Crud! Connor hoped nobody else in the chat room had caught his slipup. At least Kerri had signed off moments before Kevin logged on. Connor turned on his instant messenger. Kevin was already there.

What's up? Kevin typed.

Not much. Bored as usual.

No. What's up with the MTcwboy89 thing?

He wanted to lie. To claim it wasn't him who had responded to Kevin's message. But they were best friends. He knew he could trust Kevin with anything.

No big deal. Just trying to impress some girl.

Now I get it. Who is she?

Again, he started to avoid telling his buddy the truth. But the IM was private. No one else could see what he keyed.

Kerri Hendricks. She's CanChaser1.

I thought so. She's hot!

Yeah. Mega hot.

They chatted back and forth, Connor steering the conversation away from Kerri. He looked at the clock. His dad would be home soon.

Gotta go, dude.

OK. Later.

Connor shut down the computer, knowing what his dad would've said had he caught him again.

No chat rooms. No IM. Just e-mail.

Right.

Grumpy, Connor went to the living room and put in a DVD.

He had a date with the prettiest girl in Sage Bend. Or rather, some cowboy in Wyoming had a date with her. *Great.*

What the hell did he do now?

DERRICK SWUNG BY the drive-up window of the burger joint once the band's final set for the night was over. Tonight had been fantastic, with his mom at the Spur, listening to him play. He'd felt as if he were a kid again, showing off on stage for her.

"What would you like, Mom?"

"Nothing, thank you," Carolyn said. "My teeth are floating from all those ginger ales."

Derrick ordered a chocolate shake, plus a malt and French fries to take home to Connor. "That boy's always hungry," he said.

Carolyn laughed. "You were the same way, growing up…. Where does the time go? It seems like yesterday you were Connor's age."

"I know." His son's childhood had already passed too quickly. Derrick wanted to be sure he made the most of Connor's teen years. And he wasn't scoring big in that department after today's fiasco.

On impulse, Derrick pressed the drive-up speaker again and ordered a strawberry shake. He had no idea if she even liked strawberry…but it went with her hair.

"Another milkshake?" Carolyn arched one brow. "For you or Connor?"

"It's for Kara."

"Ah." Carolyn nodded. Propping one elbow on the armrest, she rested her cheek against her hand. "She's a very pretty girl."

"Really? I hadn't noticed."

Again, she laughed. "Well, I'm glad to see you still have your sense of humor." Her expression turned serious. "Derrick, I really don't want to cause any trouble for you with your father. Maybe I should just get a motel room. That way if Vernon drives down here—"

"Don't be silly. You're staying at my house, and that's that. If Dad comes down, we'll deal with him together."

But his father wouldn't come. Instead, he'd take it out on Carolyn when she got back. Derrick couldn't let that happen. One way or another, he'd have to face his father. He was the one who deserved Vernon's wrath—not his mother.

When Derrick pulled in to his driveway and saw the lights off at Kara's place, he was more disappointed than he cared to admit. Then he realized one light was on. Her bedroom? The thought of Kara lying alone on crisp sheets… This wasn't a game. He wanted a woman he couldn't have.

So why had he bothered to bring her a shake?

Connor was still up, watching a movie, Taz curled in his lap. "Here you go," Derrick said, handing him the paper sack of food.

"What's this?"

"A peace offering."

Taz sniffed the bag, whiskers twitching.

"Thanks." Connor eased the cat off his lap. He slid a fry into his mouth, then dumped the rest onto a paper napkin, and doused them with ketchup. The greasy potatoes soaked through the napkin to the coffee table, and Carolyn cringed.

"You want a plate?" she asked Connor.

"Sure, Grandma. Thanks."

She disappeared into the kitchen, and Derrick loved the way she already felt at home here. His mother had given Connor a basic explanation of why she'd come. She'd felt the two of them should talk to him together, when things were calmed down.

Derrick decided now wasn't the time, at such a late hour. But he wanted Connor to know what had happened to Rex, and why Connor's grandfather had written Derrick out of his life.

"I got a shake for Kara, too," Derrick said. "I'm going to run over and see if she's still awake."

Connor nodded.

Shake in hand, Derrick jogged across the street. It was almost midnight. What was he doing? Kara was probably asleep, in spite of the lighted window. He'd knock once, and if she didn't answer, he'd put the milk shake in his freezer until later.

He tiptoed onto the porch—some feat in cowboy boots—and knocked softly on the door.

KARA AWOKE to the sound of Lady growling. She sat up, dumping the paperback she'd been reading onto the floor. Disoriented, she squinted against the glow of the bedside lamp, and fumbled for the book. "What's the matter, Lady?" Sudden panic gripped her as Kara looked at the clock. *Connor.* Something must've happened.

Kara shoved one leg into her jeans, already headed for the door. She fumbled with the zipper, pausing long enough to peek through the glass at the front porch. *Derrick?* She flipped the light on and unbolted the door.

"Hi," he greeted her. "Did you fall asleep in your clothes?"

Self-consciously, Kara raked both hands over her hair. She must look a mess. "Uh, yeah, I did. Nothing's wrong, is it? Is Connor all right?"

"He's fine." Derrick held up a paper bag. "I brought you a milk shake." In his other hand, he held a foam cup with a straw sticking out of the lid.

She stared at him. "At midnight?"

He blushed. "I guess I forgot that everybody's not a night owl. I'm a rude SOB. I'll come back later." He turned to go.

"Hey, crazy man, you've already woken me up," Kara said. "You might as well come on in." She held the door wide.

He filled the doorway as he stepped inside, looking so yummy in his band getup, Kara nearly melted into a mindless puddle. She took the bag from him, examining the clear lid on the cup inside of it.

"Strawberry?"

"For a strawberry-blonde." Derrick's mouth crooked at the corners, making his dimples crease his cheeks.

Kara wanted to devour him. She had to stop this. She was a total floozy. "Um, I'm allergic to strawberries."

"You're kidding."

She shook her head. "I break out in hives."

He groaned. "I'm sorry."

"No, it was really sweet of you." She touched his arm. "It's the thought that counts, even at midnight, right?"

He held up his own cup in offering. "Want to trade? Mine's chocolate."

Kara looked at the cup, with its red-and-white-striped straw. The thought of putting her mouth where Derrick's had been…the thought of tasting him… She shivered.

"Are you cold?" He frowned. "I thought it felt pretty warm out tonight."

Kara took the nearly full shake from him, telling herself she was only being polite. "Must be the ice cream." She handed the strawberry one to him, still remembering the way his mouth had tasted.

She wanted to kiss him again. Instead, she took a sip. It was only her imagination making her think she could taste Derrick's lips. "Want to sit down for a minute?"

"Yeah, if you're sure I'm not keeping you up."

He had no idea.

"Not at all. I just fell asleep reading. I wanted to be handy if Connor needed anything."

"I appreciate that."

He sat on the sofa, and she dropped onto the opposite end. "So, how's your mom doing?"

"Fine." He smiled, and her heartbeat raced. "I can't believe she's here, after all this time."

"I'm glad she's coming around," Kara said. "So, she's feeling all right after her surgery?"

"She seems to be. Thank God it wasn't cancer, but I guess it got her thinking about how life is too short."

Kara's emotions took a dive. And suddenly, she

focused on her wedding photo across the room on the entertainment center. "That's for sure," she said, lowering her gaze.

To her chagrin, Derrick slid across the sofa until his knee was touching hers. "I'm sorry, Kara." He caressed her face. "I didn't mean to bring back bad memories."

"You didn't." That was the problem. Her memories of Evan were wonderful. She doubted she'd ever be able to stop comparing other men to him—even Derrick, as kind and handsome as he was.

The silence lay thick between them. Derrick set his cup down on a coaster. She held her breath.

"Kara, I want to kiss you."

Her heart thudded. "We shouldn't."

He paused, his hand on her shoulder. He laced it through her hair, letting the strands slide between his fingers. "Why not? Didn't you enjoy kissing me today?"

"You mean yesterday."

He waited. "Didn't you?"

"Yes. And that's why we can't do it again." She pushed his hand away and stood.

Derrick rose to his feet as well, still close. "Come on, Kara. Don't beat yourself up that way."

"Beat myself up?" She stared at him. "I'm not doing anything to myself, Derrick. Good ol' fate took care of that for me."

His eyes softened, and he reached for her again. "Kara. Fate can be cruel—I know that. But maybe fate also brought us together."

Kara remained silent.

"I want to kiss you," Derrick went on, "hold you. I want to see where things lead us."

"I told you, I'm not ready." She trembled.

He let his hand drop, clearly disappointed. "All right. I'm not going to force myself on you. Just promise me something."

"What?"

"That when you are ready to try again, you'll give me a chance."

"I can't promise you anything." How could she, when she couldn't even promise herself she'd ever be able to love again?

Derrick picked up his drink. "Guess I'd better let you get some sleep."

He walked to the door, and Kara groped for something to say. She didn't want to hurt him, but she couldn't help it. She was hurting far more deeply than he could imagine. "Thanks for the shake."

"You're welcome. Thanks for keeping an eye on Connor."

"Anytime. Good night." Kara closed the door.

Tears stung her eyes. Damn it! She was so confused. She wanted Derrick. She cared about him. But she still loved Evan. She sank to the floor and folded her arms on her knees, dropping her forehead on them. *What was she going to do?*

Liz's word echoed in her mind. *It doesn't look right...I don't want to see you get hurt.*

Kara blinked back the tears. No more crying. She'd made up her mind.

She flicked off the porch light and headed to bed. She had to stop seeing Derrick, stop stringing him along.

Her heart belonged to Evan.

CHAPTER TWELVE

THE RICH AROMA of bacon and coffee drifted through the hallway, an invisible finger beckoning Derrick toward the kitchen. The table was set, with a note propped against the salt and pepper shakers.

> Derrick,
> I can't tell you what a wonderful time I've had with you and Connor (I loved hearing you play at the Silver Spur), but I think it's best if I go home before your father causes trouble. I called and told him I'm on my way. Don't worry. It'll all work out. I'll be in touch.
> Love,
> Mom
> P.S. Breakfast is warming in the oven.

"Where's Grandma?"

Derrick looked up to see Connor in the kitchen doorway. "She went home. Didn't want to make your grandpa any madder."

"Oh." Connor rolled up to the table. "Do I smell bacon?"

"I think so." Derrick opened the oven, and removed the covered casserole dishes his mother had left. "Looks like we've got bacon, eggs and pancakes."

"Awesome. I'm starving."

Derrick laughed, laying a couple of potholders on the table. "As usual." He set the dishes down on them, and Connor helped himself.

Derrick poured orange juice and coffee. "So, Kara told me she drove you past God's Little Acre Friday."

"Yeah." Connor stuffed an entire slice of bacon into his mouth, crunching it with relish.

"I went out there with her while you were at your mom's house."

"She told me." He spoke around the bacon.

Derrick let his son's manners slide. "It looked like a pretty nice place. You sure you don't want to go check it out?"

Connor shrugged. "I dunno—maybe." He grinned crookedly. "How about if you don't ground me from my computer for driving Kara's truck, I'll go check out the riding center?"

Derrick chuckled. "All right. But you have to promise to give it a fair shot."

"Can Kara go with us?"

After last night, he wasn't so sure that was a good

idea. But he didn't want to do anything to discourage his son, and Kara had said to let her know if Connor changed his mind.

"I don't see why not. We'll call her after breakfast."

Connor cleaned up the dishes later, and after talking to Melanie Spencer on the phone, Derrick dialed Kara's number. She answered cheerfully on the first ring.

"You're awake, I see."

"Of course. It's almost ten-thirty."

"I was wondering—Connor was wondering—would you like to go out to the riding center with us?"

"You talked him in to giving it a try? Derrick, that's great."

"Well, we worked out a deal of sorts. Let's just say you and your truck had something to do with it."

She giggled. Girlish. Playful. He wished he could take her out on a real date. Maybe a picnic...

"Hey, whatever it takes. Is your mom going, too?"

"No. She left this morning."

"Oh. I haven't been outside yet."

"I already called Melanie," he said. "Can you be ready in about twenty minutes?"

"I'm ready now."

"We'll pick you up."

"Thanks. I'd hate to have to walk such a long way to your house."

The teasing note in her voice lifted his hopes.

"We can't have pretty women walking the streets in this dangerous city. See you in a few."

He hung up, anxious to see her. She hadn't come to the Spur all weekend, and neither had her friends. Was he wasting his time? It didn't matter. He'd gladly wait as long as she needed him to, for her to get over Evan.

But what if she doesn't?

Derrick refused to listen to the nagging doubt. He was falling in love with Kara and, fool or not, he was finally willing to lay his heart on the line.

KARA CHECKED HER REFLECTION in the mirror as she rebrushed her hair. Leaning closer, she frowned at her freckles, then put on some pale pink lip gloss.

What was she doing?

Sighing, she laid the tube of gloss on the sink. It didn't matter if she had makeup on or not, because she was going for Connor's sake, not Derrick's. At least that's what she kept telling herself. She ought to listen to reason and do exactly as she'd vowed— stay away from him. But she cared about Connor.

She also didn't want to admit she'd played dumb to Derrick. She'd known his mother was gone. She'd looked out the window first thing that morning, to see if her car was still in the driveway.

She'd told Derrick she wasn't ready to move on, but she needed to make him see why. Without hurting his feelings. He was a nice guy. He just wasn't the guy for her. Or more accurately, she wasn't the woman for him.

Right on time, Derrick pulled the truck into her driveway. Kara squeezed into the cab beside Connor. "Hi there. Changed your mind after all, huh?"

He shrugged. "I guess it won't hurt to go see the place."

"That's the spirit." She avoided Derrick's gaze, feeling tense in the close space of the small truck, re-membering the last time she'd been here with him, and how he'd sang to her. All the way to the center, she made idle chitchat, trying to keep her thoughts in check.

But when Melanie took them for their second tour, all Kara could focus on was the way Derrick interacted with his son. She watched as he followed Connor, cracking jokes, doing his best to whet his son's interest, yet not pushing the boy. Derrick's tone and body language said far more than his actual words—that whether Connor chose to ride or not was ultimately his decision.

Kara appreciated that he wasn't trying to push horseback riding on Connor just because he'd enjoyed it as a boy. That Derrick was only out to help his son hit her hard, and suddenly Kara wanted to cry. Why had she and Evan waited to have children?

She could've had a child—a part of Evan—to love and raise.

What if Connor were her and Derrick's son? What if she and Derrick had a child together? She pictured it. They'd all have horses, Connor having learned to ride at God's Little Acre. They'd spend every weekend horseback riding, and Danita, Hannah and Beth would sometimes join them.

Then at night, Derrick would tuck their child in bed and read her a story, while Kara helped Connor with last-minute homework. With the kids in bed, she and Derrick would curl up in each other's arms, making plans for the future that included buying a ranch of their own....

Where would we live meanwhile? Certainly not in the house she'd shared with Evan. And not in Derrick's little mint-green house across the street. No way could she look over at her old home every day and remember....

"Ah. Here comes Lisa."

Melanie's voice jolted Kara back to reality. They'd arrived at God's Little Acre. She looked up to see the young girl she and Connor had driven past on Friday, riding the flashy black-and-white Paint.

"Lisa," Melanie said, waving her over. "I've got somebody I'd like you to meet."

Lisa nudged the gelding forward, her attention on Connor.

Kara hid a smile, noting the expression on Connor's face. No two ways about it, the boy had it bad. His eyes followed Lisa's every move as she walked the Paint closer to the hitching post next to the mounting ramp.

Then she slid from the saddle, and reached for the pair of aluminum crutches leaning against the post.

Connor's jaw dropped as Kara checked her own reaction. Lisa slipped her arms into the supportive cuffs on each crutch, then swung over to sit on a bench just feet away. Only then did Kara notice the leg braces lying there. Lisa slipped them on while her horse stood patiently waiting, reins looped over the hitching post. Then she walked over to join the group.

"Hi," she said, smiling at Connor. "I'm Lisa."

"C-Connor." He blushed, unable to stop staring at her.

Melanie made a round of introductions. "Lisa is our youngest volunteer," she said. "She's the young lady I was telling you and Kara about the other day, Derrick."

"Nice to meet you, Lisa," Derrick said. "That's quite a horse you've got there."

"Thanks." Lisa's face lit up. "His name is Maverick, but he's actually a big baby."

Derrick chuckled. "Does he belong to the riding center?"

"No, he's mine," Lisa said. "My parents bought him from Melanie."

"We try to keep our eye out for extra horses to purchase now and then," Melanie said. "In case any of our students want a horse of their own." She looked at Connor. "So, buddy, what do you think? Want to give us a whirl? We'd love to do an evaluation with you once your dad gets the forms back from Doctor Sorenson."

"Sure," Connor said, suddenly enthusiastic. "Sounds good to me."

Derrick clapped his son on the back. "Glad to hear it." He beamed at Connor, then met Kara's gaze and grinned.

She smiled back, his joy contagious. "Smart choice."

But Connor only had eyes for Lisa.

With a promise from Derrick to get back to Melanie to set up an appointment, they said their goodbyes. In the truck, Connor craned his neck to look out the back window as they pulled away.

"She's pretty," Kara said.

"Yeah, I'd say." Connor faced forward. "I can't believe she was riding like that."

"What do you mean?" Derrick asked.

"You know, like a normal kid. Lisa didn't even look handicapped until she got off her horse."

"Surprised me, too," Derrick said.

Kara had to admit, her reaction had been the same. "See," she said. "I told you you'd be able to ride."

His face fell slightly. "Yeah, but Lisa's not paralyzed. What if I can't stay in the saddle?"

"You will," Derrick said. "Heck, if those little kids can do it, you can."

KARA GOT HER TRUCK back from the shop on Wednesday, and was impressed with the bodywork. The shop's owner had managed to find an original grill off a '78 Ford pickup, and had rechromed and installed it once the radiator had been replaced. Kara couldn't even tell it wasn't the one she'd ruined.

On Friday, Derrick called to invite her to watch Connor's evaluation. July had brought higher temperatures, so he'd set up an early morning appointment with Melanie when it would still be cool outside.

"Are you sure I won't make Connor nervous?" Kara asked.

"He wants you to come," Derrick said.

She couldn't help but wonder if it were really Derrick who wanted her there. She wouldn't let her seesawing emotions interfere with Connor's big day, so Kara accepted the invitation.

"We'll leave here at seven," Derrick said. "I'm looking forward to it, Kara."

"See you then." She hung up the phone, wondering if his emphasis had been on seeing her or helping his son.

The next morning, Kara awoke to gray skies and a light sprinkle that turned into a drizzling rain by the time Derrick and Connor picked her up.

"Great," Connor said, scowling at the clouds. "How am I supposed to ride in the rain?"

"Didn't Melanie tell you?" Kara deadpanned. "She's got custom raingear for the riders and the horses, including a giant umbrella you hold over your saddle and your horse's head."

"Really?" Connor frowned.

"Oh, yeah. And they attach flipper fins to the horseshoes, in case the puddles get too deep."

"Right." Connor shot her a grin.

Derrick laughed, and Kara was suddenly acutely aware of the warmth among the three of them—a warmth that dispelled the chill outside.

"They've got an indoor arena," Derrick said.

This time Kara laughed, despite feeling like a traitor for having so much fun.

Connor looked nervous once they'd parked.

"Don't worry," Kara said. "You'll do fine."

He shrugged. But his eyes lit up when Melanie showed the three of them to the indoor arena.

Lisa Owens was there, putting her Paint horse through an obstacle course at an easy lope. She looked so graceful in the saddle, and Kara marveled at how different the girl on the horse was from the one who needed crutches and leg braces to get around on the ground.

"Connor, this is Lollipop," Melanie said, laying her hand on the shoulder of a liver chestnut gelding. The horse was only about fourteen hands high.

"Lollipop?" Connor smirked.

"He's a real sweetie—just like his name—so don't be nervous."

"Yeah, okay."

But Connor kept one eye on Lisa. Kara wondered if the girl's presence was a good thing or not. Either it would make Connor all the more self-conscious, or it would give him the gumption to show off for a pretty girl.

"I think someone's got a crush," Derrick said softly as they sat in the bleachers, watching Melanie and two volunteer assistants take Connor to the mounting ramp.

Kara met his gaze. His eyes were dancing with a sort of happiness that made her spirits soar. "I think so, too," she said. "Lisa's a cutie."

"Yes, she is. And I owe her a debt of gratitude. I don't think Connor would've agreed to give this place a try if he hadn't been smitten."

She chuckled. "I kind of noticed that. But hey—whatever works, right?"

"Yeah." His expression softened. "Kara, would

you like to go to the Spur tonight with us? Connor deserves a fun night out."

Kara opened her mouth to say no. Then, out of the corner of her eye, she saw Connor, sitting on Lollipop's back.

"Dad, look!" he called, then as though realizing showing off for his dad was beneath a fourteen-year-old, added, "Look how nice Lollipop moves."

"I see that," Derrick said. "He's a great horse."

"Yeah!" Melanie led the horse while the two side-walkers steadied Connor in the saddle.

But they soon realized there wasn't a whole lot of need. Connor had a knack for sitting the gelding and, disabled or not, he rode with quiet ease. His strong upper body flexed, keeping his torso in the proper position, his shoulders helping him balance.

Kara got a sudden lump in her throat. "Look at him," she said. "It's like he can walk again."

"Yeah." Derrick's focus was totally on his son.

Kara watched as tears filled Derrick's eyes. She saw him swallow—hard. And when Lisa dropped in beside Connor and rode with him, making the boy laugh and chat like she'd never seen him do before, Derrick slipped his arm around Kara's shoulders.

"I've never seen him this happy." He leaned over and brushed a kiss across Kara's lips. "Will you go with us tonight?"

She nodded.

He squeezed her shoulders, still holding her. "Thank you for making this happen."

Kara's breath caught. "I didn't do anything," she mumbled.

"He wouldn't be here if you hadn't brought up the idea. I can't thank you enough." He kissed her again, then pulled away, dropping his arm from her shoulders.

Kara sat on her hands to keep from touching her lips. Her mouth felt on fire.

"You're welcome," she said.

CHAPTER THIRTEEN

DERRICK FELT LIKE a teenager getting ready for a date. He'd put on his best shirt, his new Wranglers, and he'd steam-cleaned and shaped his cowboy hat. Still, he stared at the mirror wondering what Kara would see when she looked at him. He wanted her to see a man who was falling in love with her, a man who could share her life and make her happy.

His entire life, he'd never handled relationships well. Not with his son, not with Shelly, not with his own parents.

He kept trying to make things right, trying to convince himself he was worthy of Kara. And tonight he had no guitar to hide behind. His only crutch was his son, and he felt shamed for even thinking that way.

Thank God for Lisa Owens and Melanie Spencer and Kara, who had made horseback riding a possibility for Connor. Why hadn't he thought of the freedom and independence horseback riding could bring his son?

No matter. They were on the right track now. He

would enjoy the evening out with his son and Kara. She'd made it clear she wasn't ready for anything beyond friendship.

He'd have to settle for that.

Derrick slipped on his black cowboy hat, narrowing his eyes at his reflection.

So get over her already.

Maybe if he said the words over and over, he'd be able to do just that.

CONNOR PUT ON a clean shirt, his hands damp, not from the shower, but from nervous sweat. He'd been so wrapped up in thinking about Lisa all afternoon he'd practically forgotten Kerri Hendricks would be at the Silver Spur tonight.

So here he was, getting ready for a celebration with his dad and Kara, when suddenly he didn't feel so much like celebrating after all. Sure, Kerri would have no way of knowing who he really was, but just seeing her at the Spur was gonna be tough. Wanting what he couldn't have sucked.

Connor combed his hair, then shoved a ball cap over it. What the hell did it matter?

"IT FEELS STRANGE to be on this side of the stage." Derrick sat next to Kara at a table close to the bandstand. "I feel naked without my guitar."

His cheeks dimpled, and Kara told herself for the

thousandth time that she could get through this evening. She laughed, not letting her imagination take her places it shouldn't. "I'm sure."

"We're here for Connor tonight, right, buddy?"

"Dad, you really don't need to make such a big deal out of everything," Connor said, rolling his eyes at Kevin, who he'd asked to come with them at the last minute.

"Well, it is a big deal," Kara said, nudging him with her elbow. "Maybe I'll even bring Indio over to the center sometime and challenge you to a race."

"Yeah, right." Connor snorted. "It wouldn't be much of one."

"Are you insulting my horse?" She feigned indignation.

"If we raced, you'd leave me in the dust—literally."

Kara glanced at Derrick—his face had paled and he'd set his mouth in a grim line. Instantly, she realized where his thoughts must have gone. She opened her mouth to apologize, then decided it would only make matters worse.

"I doubt it," she said lightly. "Hey, I hope you two don't mind, but I asked my friends to join us tonight." With each call to Danita, Beth and Hannah, she'd felt as if she'd added one more protective barrier between her and her growing feelings for Derrick.

"Not at all," Derrick said, his features returning to normal. "We'll make it a party."

"Here comes Beth and Hannah now."

Danita joined the group a half hour later, and within minutes, the band started up. Soon Kara was lost in the fun of line dancing. So much so, that at first she didn't notice the group of kids who came in and sat down at the next table. Not until she'd left the dance floor did she see the three boys who'd taunted Connor in the parking lot the night he fell. Kara hadn't forgotten their hateful faces.

They were with the same two girls tonight as well, plus a pretty blonde with waist-length hair, who looked familiar. She wriggled her skinny butt as she headed for the dance floor with the boy who'd been meanest to Connor, casting a smug look over her shoulder at him. Connor's face reddened, and he looked away, reaching for the nachos Derrick had ordered.

"Ignore them," Kevin said, elbowing him in the side.

"I am."

Danita looked puzzled, and Kara discreetly mouthed "Later."

Distracted, she was caught off guard when Derrick took her by the hand. "Come on. Let's dance." He tugged her to her feet.

Kara froze. "Thanks, but—"

"No excuses," he said. "I promise I won't bite."

"Go on, Kara," Hannah urged, giving her a crooked smile, "before I decide to steal your handsome cowboy."

Kara opened her mouth to protest that Derrick wasn't hers, but he silenced her by slipping an arm around her waist and guiding her out onto the polished, hardwood floor. Belatedly, she realized the band had switched to a slow love song.

"Derrick, I don't think this is such a good idea." She looked directly into his eyes as he tugged her up against him.

"Why not?" He swayed to the music, matching his hips against hers. "We're here to have fun, Kara. Just dance with me." His eyes begged her to give in.

Unable to resist, Kara sighed. "All right. Just one." She leaned her head on his shoulder, tense.

"Relax," he whispered against her hair. She felt him brush a kiss on the top of her head.

After a moment, she let out a breath and felt herself relax. It felt so good to be held. Kara closed her eyes and eased into the rhythm of the music, and the sway of her body against Derrick's. His arms felt warm and strong, and oh, so comforting. She fought the tightness in her throat. She wasn't doing anything wrong.

"You smell so sweet," he said, the words tickling her ear…her senses.

"So do you," she answered automatically. "I mean, not sweet, but good." *Damn!*

He chuckled. "What's wrong, Kara? You seem rattled."

She was rattled all right. "I'm fine." Still leaning against Derrick, she looked around. Were people staring? Was that Lily Tate, with a plate of barbecue ribs, two tables away? Did she notice Kara in the arms of a man who wasn't Evan? *Dear God,* there was Liz, not twenty feet away!

Kara almost jumped out of her skin before she realized it was only someone with short hair wearing a shirt similar to the one Liz had worn the other night.

Stop it.

Kara's pulse raced as Derrick picked that moment to sing along with the music. Softly. She let herself forget everything, except how it felt to dance with a man she'd fallen in love with. Lord help her, she could no longer deny it, and she truly couldn't help what she felt.

Unconsciously, Kara slid her palm along Derrick's warm back. His muscles were hard beneath her touch. The fabric of his shirt soft and inviting. She wanted to feel his bare skin. Wanted to press her body even closer. The song ended, and he leaned down to kiss her. Kara kissed him back, their tongues touching briefly.

"See—that wasn't so bad," he said. His lips curved, and he laced his fingers through hers as they headed for their table.

Danita mouthed "Go, girl" as Kara sat down. Maybe there wasn't any harm in enjoying a dance with Derrick.

"Thanks," Derrick said, holding Kara's chair for her.

"I'm wounded," Connor said, clutching both hands to his chest. "I thought I was your only dance partner, Kara."

She laughed, glad he'd broken the tension. "You're next," she said, "then you, Kevin."

Connor started to cuff his friend in the shoulder when his gaze focused on a point beyond Kara. "Hey, there's Lisa." His eyes lit up. "I've never seen her here before."

Kara turned and saw her, leaning on her crutches beside a short, round woman with silver-blond hair. Lisa waved at Connor and smiled as she sat at the table a waitress had led them to.

"That's Kay Owens with her," Hannah said. "Lisa's aunt. I take care of their horses. I've seen the two stop here for dinner on occasion."

Kara started to ask Hannah why she hadn't mentioned Lisa before, but just then someone spoke at her elbow.

"Hey, Connor."

It was the pretty blonde in the low-rider jeans. She stood between Kara's chair and Danita's, leaning over the table in a way that gave Connor a prime view of her cleavage. Kevin's eyes were practically bulging out of his head.

Connor swallowed. "H-hey, Kerri. What's up?"

"Not much," she said, quirking her pretty mouth in a flirty pout. "I'm just here to meet somebody."

"Yeah? I, uh, thought you were with Bart." He glanced over at the tall, dark-haired boy.

"Not tonight." With a toss of her head, Kerri flipped her long hair over her shoulder.

"Who's your friend, Connor?" Derrick asked.

Kara suddenly realized why the girl looked familiar. She was Kerri Hendricks. Her father had money, and Kerri drove a truck that probably cost more than Kara's house.

"Hi," Kerri said to Derrick, flirting like crazy. "You're the lead singer of Wild Country, aren't you?"

"That's right. I'm Connor's dad." He held out his hand, and Kerri gave it a prim shake, then turned back to Connor.

"I'm here to meet a rodeo cowboy, Connor. From Billings."

"So, why are you telling me?" His gaze dropped to the glass of Coke in front of him.

The band picked that moment to go on break,

and in the lull between the end of their set and the time it took someone to fire up the jukebox, Kara heard laughter from the next table where Bart and his buddies sat.

What were they up to?

She narrowed her eyes at Kerri. But the girl ignored her, continuing her little game.

"Maybe you know him," Kerri said. "I'm pretty sure Kevin does."

Kevin frowned, puzzled. "I know a couple of guys from Billings, but neither of them rodeo."

"Oh, I think you know this guy." Kerri gave them a saccharine smile, then pulled a folded piece of paper out of the back pocket of her skintight jeans.

Kara was surprised she could even get her hand inside the pocket. She watched Connor's face as Kerri opened the paper to reveal a printed photo of a good-looking kid in western clothes, a black cowboy hat tilted at a cocky angle.

"Look familiar?" she asked. "Montana Cowboy eighty-nine." This last she said as though addressing Connor.

A burst of laughter made Kara look at the next table again. Kerri's friends were watching, clearly enjoying this.

"Yee-haw," Bart called. "Ride 'em, cowboy." The others laughed even louder, staring at Connor as they relished his humiliation.

"What's going on here?" Derrick looked from Connor to Kerri.

But Connor ignored his dad, facing Kevin instead, his expression furious. "You idiot!"

"What?" Kevin stared blankly at him for a moment. "I didn't say anything! I swear."

"Your secret's out, Mertz," Bart taunted, "you little faggot. You wish you could ride a bull!"

"I *said*, what's going on?" Derrick repeated.

"Nothing, Mr. Mertz," Kerri said sweetly as she turned away. "Nothing at all."

"The only thing you'll ever ride is that chair," one of the other boys called.

"Hey." Kara stood. "That's enough."

"Shut up." Connor thrust his wheelchair away from the table. His face was twisted with fury as he stared down Bart and his buddies. "Just shut the hell up, you assholes!" Then he reached out and shoved Kevin's shoulder, nearly tipping him out of his chair. "I thought you were my friend. Thanks a lot."

"Connor." Derrick stared at his son.

"Leave me alone." Connor spun around, nearly bowling down Lisa, who'd come up to the table. He stared right past her and headed for the back of the bar.

CHAPTER FOURTEEN

DERRICK GOT UP to go after him.

"No," Kara said, laying her hand on his shoulder, "let me." Her eyes met his. "Please. He doesn't want his daddy running after him."

"Maybe you shouldn't, either," Beth said. "Besides, I think he's headed for the bathroom."

"I'll wait outside the door, then," Kara said, hurrying away before Derrick could protest.

Leaning against the wall just outside the doorway of the men's room, Kara waited until it was obvious Connor wasn't coming out. When she was pretty sure all the cowboys who'd passed by her on the way in had also passed by on the way out, Kara walked hesitantly inside.

"Connor? Are you okay?"

"Leave me alone."

"Unless you're planning to spend the night in there, you have to come out sooner or later." Silence. "Come on, buddy, talk to me. We can go outside if you want."

Connor wheeled past her out of the men's room. His eyes were red, but he'd obviously fought the urge to cry. Kara was sure he felt beyond embarrassed.

She laid her hand on his shoulder. "Come on." She jerked her head toward a side exit.

They found a quiet place in the parking lot. "You don't have to explain what just happened back there, unless you want to." Kara propped her booted foot on a cement parking barrier. "But whatever it was, why do you let those jerks get to you like that? It's exactly what they want, you know—to yank your chain."

"I'm never going back in there again." Connor blinked angrily, wiping his nose with the back of his hand. "I've never felt so damned stupid in my life. *God!* I can't even trust my best friend."

"Whoa, back up a minute." She stared directly at him. "Are you sure you're not jumping to conclusions? Like I said, I don't know what's going on, but Kevin didn't seem to, either. I saw his face. He wasn't lying to you."

"There's no other way Kerri could've known…. Forget it. I just want to go home."

"Fine," Kara said. "We can do that. Or, you can go back in there and face those little jackasses and show them what you're made of."

Connor's eyes narrowed. "What do you mean?"

"Hear that?" She jerked her head toward the building.

"What—the band?"

"That's right. It's not your dad's band, but they are friends of his, right?"

"He knows them, yeah. So?"

"Go back in there, pull the lead singer aside, and ask him if you can play a song."

"Are you nuts? No way!"

"Why? Connor, I'm sorry, but I don't understand why you don't want your dad to know what a great guitar player—and singer—you are. What gives?"

He stared at his cowboy boots, and for a minute, Kara thought he wasn't going to answer.

"You saw how those girls laughed at me," he finally said. "And stupid-ass Bart Denson." He sighed. "I went online in a chat room, and pretended to be a bull rider. I was trying to impress Kerri. Kevin must've told her."

"What makes you think it was Kevin?"

"Because he was the only one I told."

"You're sure no one else knew?"

"Yeah. I didn't even mean to tell *him*. I was logged on under the wrong screen name, and—" He broke off, frowning. "Crap. Maybe he didn't say anything. Kerri was online right before that, and I slipped up and answered Kevin without switching to my real screen name, which everyone knows. Then I did switch, and I kept chatting with Kevin."

"Kerri."

"Yeah. Man!" He groaned and yanked his ball cap low over his eyes. "Lisa probably thinks I'm a real jerk now. I practically ran over her. How am I supposed to face her at the riding center?"

"You're not. You face her here, now—and Bart and Kerri and their friends, too."

"By singing?"

"You got it. Chicken?" She raised her eyebrows.

He readjusted the cap. But she could see his mind racing.

"Come on. Your dad will be really surprised. It'll be cool. Lisa will melt into a puddle, and Kerri will wish she hadn't been so mean to you. I even know the perfect song, that is if you can play it." She told him what it was.

"I don't know." But he chuckled. "Jackasses, huh?"

"Well, they are."

He laughed again, worrying his bottom lip. "All right."

"Yes!" Kara clapped him on the shoulder.

But back inside the bar, Connor hesitated. "I don't know if David Miller will let me use his guitar."

"I'm betting he will."

He let his breath out on a long exhale. "Okay."

Kara watched him go over and stop at the side of the stage. Derrick spotted him and started to get up. Kara hurried to the table, motioning him to stay put.

"What's going on?" he asked. "Is Connor all right?"

"I think so. Just watch." She sat and sipped her Coke, to give her hands something to do besides shake. She was so excited for Connor, and she knew Derrick was going to be bowled over. She couldn't wait to see the look on his face.

David Miller—the lead singer of Rockin' Cowboys—stepped up to the microphone.

"Hey, everybody, are y'all havin' a good time tonight?"

"Yeah!" The crowd's collective response included whistling and cheering. Beth let out a loud whoop, and Danita put her fingers to her lips, whistling. Kevin sat quiet—he still looked hurt.

"All right," David said. "We've got a real treat for you tonight, a young man making his debut here at the Silver Spur. Y'all might know his daddy, who's a fine guitar picker—though not as good as me."

Everyone laughed, including Derrick, even though he looked puzzled.

"So, put your hands together and give a warm welcome to our own Connor Mertz!"

The crowd cheered and roared, applauding loudly. Kara caught a glimpse of the surprise on Kerri Hendricks's face, as well as Bart Denson's and the rest of his bratty bunch. Derrick laid his hand on her arm. The expression on his face was priceless.

"What's he doing?" His mouth gaped slightly.

"Watch and see." Kara grinned at Danita.

"I didn't know Connor played the guitar, Derrick," Hannah said.

Derrick sat up straighter in his chair. "Neither did I."

CONNOR FELT yet another moment of humiliation as the drummer and the keyboard player hefted him up the four steps to the stage. But he didn't have long to think about it as David shrugged out of his guitar strap, and handed him the Fender. "It's all yours, son," he said softly. "Give 'em hell."

Hands shaking, Connor took the guitar. He'd worried about the microphone—that it wouldn't adjust low enough for his chair. But David gave him a headset microphone, and Connor clipped it on, then replaced his ball cap. Glad he'd worn a rad T-shirt and his best jeans, he faced the audience. The stage lights felt hot on his face, and he began to sweat immediately. He was going to make a fool of himself. He just knew it. He could barely make out his dad and Kara for the glare of the lights.

Blocking everything from his mind, Connor ran a short warm-up lick on the guitar, then spoke into the microphone. And it was as he saw Lisa looking at him, a smile on her pretty lips, that his hands stopped shaking.

"Hey, y'all. I'd like to dedicate this song to a certain someone in the audience." He cast a dark look toward Kerri's table. "You know who you are." He glanced at Kara, and she gave a nearly imperceptible nod.

Connor began to play. The more he got into the song, the more confident he felt. He let his voice rise on the chorus of his rendition of Toby Keith's "How Do You Like Me Now"—a song about a girl who won't give a boy the time of day in high school. A boy who later becomes a recording star.

The music swept him away, and he forgot about his wheelchair, his humiliation, until he no longer gave a damn what Kerri thought of him.

When he'd finished, he raked the pick across the strings on the final note and shouted, "Yeah!"

The audience exploded. Not only that, they gave him a standing ovation. A friggin' *standing ovation!* He couldn't have planned it better if he'd dreamed up a fantasy.

"All right!" David clapped loudly as he walked back up to the microphone stand. "There he is, folks! Connor Mertz."

Connor felt on top of the world. He shrugged out of the guitar strap and handed the Fender back to

David. Then he took off the headset. "Thanks, dude," he said, loud enough only for David to hear.

"Anytime, bud." David turned to the crowd. "We've got another hour left of family night, folks, so let's keep things rolling."

But Connor barely heard the rest of what he said, as the guys lowered him back down the steps. He was flying. Hell, he felt like he could jump out of his chair—jump out of his own skin. Kara had thought of the perfect song.

"Eat that shithead," he said as he passed Bart's table.

"Faggot hick," Bart shot back.

Connor reached up and high-fived Kevin, and his buddy grinned, accepting his unspoken apology.

"Ooo, you think you're so cool," Bart said. "Big time *gui*-tar picker. Yee-haw!" He and Kerri and the others laughed.

"Ignore them." Kevin shot Kerri a hateful look.

She merely folded her arms, looking down her nose at Connor.

"I don't like you now any better than I did before, Montana Cowboy," she razzed. She wriggled her hips, showing off a silver belly ring. "Come on, Bart. Let's dance to some real music."

The band had already started to play a toe-tapping, country-rock song.

The elation of moments before blew out of Connor like air from a punctured tire.

"Connor!" His dad came around the table to meet him. "My God, son, where did you learn to play like that?" He was so damned proud, Connor felt even worse.

He had thought he *was* being pretty cool.

I don't like you now any better than I did before...Montana Cowboy.

He'd made an ass of himself. As usual. And he'd jumped to conclusions about Kevin. He couldn't do anything right. And now the whole school—the whole town—would know he'd pretended to be someone he wasn't.

His stupid song hadn't changed anything.

"Way to go!" Kara said, clapping him on the back. "You were fantastic, kiddo!"

"I've gotta get out of here," he said, unable to look at Kara, his dad, her friends...and most of all Lisa, who'd come over to their table. He whirled around and headed for the exit.

"Connor!" His dad called after him.

But he kept going, a powerful black fury overwhelming him.

DERRICK AND KARA hurried after him. She'd seen Connor talking to Kerri and Bart. The boys had obviously exchanged heated words, but she'd been so sure Connor would feel one-hundred percent better. What on earth had happened?

Outside, the sun was still shining in a late evening glow. Derrick had left his pickup near the door, but Connor wasn't at the truck.

"Connor!" Derrick called, his eyes searching the parking lot.

Then Kara heard it. The sound of breaking glass.

Derrick mumbled an expletive and took off at a run. Adrenaline pumping, Kara raced after him, weaving rapidly through rows of trucks and cars to the last one, near the open field behind the Silver Spur.

Connor was there, a huge rock in his hand. And as she watched, horrified, he hurled it through the broken window of Kerri Hendricks's fancy pickup truck.

CHAPTER FIFTEEN

By the time he drove Kara home, Derrick was exhausted. He made sure she got inside the house before crossing to his own driveway. Connor sat, silent, in the passenger seat. Derrick was so angry, he didn't dare say a word for fear he'd explode.

Once inside, he spoke quietly. "Go to your room and wait for me."

Connor wheeled down the hall, his expression one of defeat. He looked as tired as Derrick felt. In the kitchen, Derrick poured himself a glass of cold water, sipping it while he gave himself time to cool off. He couldn't believe what Connor had done.

He set the glass in the sink, then knocked on Connor's bedroom door.

"It's open."

The boy was sitting on his bed, simply staring into space. The teen darted a nervous glance toward Derrick as he sat at the foot of the mattress. "Do you want to tell me why you did what you did?"

He merely shrugged.

"Connor, you're lucky Kerri's parents didn't call the police. Or Tina, either, seeing as the incident happened on her property."

"I'll pay for the window." Connor wouldn't meet his eyes.

"I know you will, I'll set up some extra chores. And you're also going to have to tell your mom what happened." Derrick raked one hand through his hair. "This probably means she won't let me take you to the Silver Spur anymore."

"I don't care!" Now Connor did look up, and his expression was one of fury and pain. "I only wanted to show you that I could sing, and play the guitar. I thought you'd be proud—that everyone would be impressed." He snorted. "How lame is that? They all laughed at me."

"Son, you can't retaliate with violence. We've been through this before. What Kerri and her friends did was awful. But you should've just walked away."

"I can't walk," Connor said deliberately.

"Don't be a smart-mouth. You know what I'm saying."

"So, is that it? I pay for her truck window? Or am I grounded from the computer, too?"

"Definitely grounded."

"For how long?"

"We'll talk about the particulars tomorrow when

I'm not so tired and ticked off." Derrick stood. "Brush your teeth and go to bed."

He left the room, utterly at a loss. What the hell would Shelly think when she found out what happened? She knew Connor had come to hear him play before, but she didn't know he'd gone to the Spur regularly. Derrick could see it now—could hear the accusations.

What's wrong with you, Derrick? What were you thinking, taking our son into a honky-tonk?

He hated not having custody of Connor—even joint custody. And he hated being told what he could and couldn't do with his own son, always having someone looking over his shoulder, judging his every move. If it wasn't Shelly and the court system, it was his own father.

He couldn't take much more.

Out on the front porch, he looked across the street. Kara's bedroom light was still on. A quick check showed Connor's was off—that he'd gone to bed. Locking the door behind him, Derrick put on his hat and walked across the street. He stood on Kara's porch, hesitating for a moment, fist poised to knock, then gave the door a rap.

Inside, Lady barked, and a moment later, Kara peered out the window. "Derrick," she said, opening the door. "What's going on?"

"Can I come in for a minute?"

"Of course." She held the door open.

They sat on her couch, and again, Derrick was all too aware of Evan's presence in the room. Absently, he petted Lady's head. "I don't know what to do anymore," he said. "Where did I go wrong?"

When you decided to put your son's life in danger, drag racing.

"Derrick." Kara laid her hand on his knee. "You're being way too hard on yourself. You're a great dad, but kids just do things. It's a normal part of being a teenager."

"Normal? Normal doesn't involve destroying someone else's property." He shook his head. "I can't believe he busted out Kerri's truck window. My God!"

"He was hurt," she said softly. "I know it's wrong, but I wanted to do something to Kerri myself—and those other brats. Like maybe put a cowboy boot up their ass."

He laughed. "Kara. I didn't know you had it in you."

She blushed, then smiled. "It's the redhead in me. I have a temper."

Derrick chuckled. "Remind me not to ever cross you."

"I don't think you need to worry about that."

"Don't be too sure. I didn't think I'd ever make my son as mad at me as he is now. And why he's mad, I don't know. I wasn't the one who threw the rocks."

"He's angry, Derrick, but not at you. Do you know how hard it was for him to get up on that stage? He wanted you to be proud of him."

"I was. I *am* proud of him." He shook his head, still at a loss. "And now I've got to punish him for what he did. I feel like I'm caught between the old rock and a hard spot."

"I'm not a parent, obviously," Kara said quietly, "but I can understand what you must be feeling."

He appreciated that more than she could know. "Normally, I would ground him from the computer. But this seems to call for something more—only I don't know what."

"You're making him make restitution, right?"

"Yeah." He sighed. "Maybe I should tell him he can't take riding lessons."

"Oh, Derrick." Kara stared at him. "You can't do that!"

"Well, I have to do something to get his attention."

"My God. After all you did—we did—to get him to agree to go? It's none of my business, but I think you're making a huge mistake."

He slouched back against the couch, staring at the ceiling. "You're probably right. Hell, Kara, I've never been a full-time parent. And I've never had to deal with anything this serious before…. Mostly, I'm worried about what Shelly will say. She'll probably drag me back to court and have my visitation revoked again."

"I don't know Shelly, but she sounds like a pretty good mom."

His cowboy hat tilted, and Kara brushed a piece of hair back from his temple. Her touch was soft…comforting.

"Surely she wouldn't do something so unreasonable," Kara continued. "What happened tonight wasn't your fault."

"I had my son in a bar."

"So did dozens of other parents. Derrick, it was *family night*. You didn't do anything wrong."

"So why do I feel so lousy about it?"

"Because you're a good father, and you want what's best for your son." She let her hand fall to her side. "You can't protect him from everything. You can't put him in bubble wrap."

"I know that." Did he? Maybe Kara had a point. Maybe he'd shielded Connor too often for too long.

"He's fourteen," Kara reminded him. "You need to give him a little credit—some space to make his own choices, good or bad. It's the only way he can learn."

"That still doesn't solve my problem. How do I punish him for what he did? How do I handle this whole situation?"

She lifted a shoulder. "Ask Shelly. Work with her to come up with something."

He sighed. "Connor's never given me much trouble before, other than the usual teenage stuff. I just feel so damned helpless!"

"I'm sure you do." She was silent a moment. "You could take away his driving privileges." Her eyes sparkled.

"Very funny."

Suddenly, Derrick was overwhelmed by Kara's nearness. By her sense of humor, her compassion and most of all just by the sight of her. He'd tried his best not to, but he'd fallen for this woman. He reached out to touch her cheek, and she froze.

But this time, he saw something else in her eyes. Something that gave him hope. Whether Kara wanted to admit it or not, she wanted him as badly as he wanted her. Life was too short not to take risks.

He leaned forward and brushed a kiss across her lips. She kissed him back, hesitantly at first, then with more enthusiasm. He cupped her face between his hands, still kissing her. "Kara," he murmured against her lips. "You taste so sweet." He thrust his tongue into her mouth, and she pulled back a little.

"Derrick, we shouldn't…"

"Why not?" He nibbled kisses across her jawline to her earlobe…her neck. "You're a woman and I'm a man, and we both want the same thing. Don't we?"

"I don't know," she whispered. But she kissed him back, deepening the kiss.

It was all he could do not to tear her clothes off and press her down on the couch.

"Kara, I want to make love to you. I want to hold you all night, and wake up with you in the morning."

She froze. "Derrick, we can't. I can't... Evan's bed..."

"Do you have a blanket?" he whispered.

Tentatively, she nodded.

"Pillows?"

"Uh-huh."

He nuzzled her neck. "Get them. Let me make you feel good, Kara."

She moaned, leaning into him. "You're making it awfully hard to say no."

"Good." He nibbled kisses against her earlobe. "That's the whole idea."

"Derrick." She drew back and looked at him, her eyes hungry...longing for him as much as he for her. She stroked his face, and for a minute, he thought he saw tears in her eyes. But she gave him a hesitant smile, then brushed a kiss across his lips. "I need this," she whispered. "But I'm scared."

"Don't be." He caressed her arms, her back, smoothing his hands over her firm body. "The blanket."

She bit her lip. Nodded. And rose from the couch. Moments later, she was back with a soft, padded quilt and two big, fluffy pillows. She tossed them on the floor between the coffee table and the leather chair, and switched off the lamp. He could still see her, silhouetted in the backlight of the streetlamps that filtered through a crack in the curtains. He took her by the hand and urged her to join him on the quilt.

She took his hat off and set it on the coffee table. "I love that hat."

"Yeah? Well, I love that blouse you're wearing—" he tucked his finger into the neckline, between the buttons "—but I'll bet it would look even better on the floor."

She laughed softly. "That's a pretty lame line, cowboy."

"I can't help it. You turn my brain to mush." He reached for her, kissing her, pressing her gently down on her back. "Kara, tell me if I do anything that makes you uncomfortable." He was on fire, and he wanted nothing more than to tear off her clothes.

"Fair enough," Kara said, reaching for the snaps on his shirt.

With every snap she unfastened, he wanted to tell her to hurry. Wanted her to pop the shirt open and quit wasting time. But he'd waited long enough to be with her. He wanted to relish every moment.

Derrick shrugged out of his shirt, and slowly undressed her. He started with that western blouse that had been teasing him all night long, giving him a glimpse of her curvy breasts. Now he saw that she wore a lacy, pale blue bra, her breasts swelling slightly above the cups.

He relished touching her, kissing her nipples, sucking them through the lace before unsnapping her bra. "You're so soft." He nuzzled the hollow of her throat…her breasts. "God, Kara, I could eat every inch of you." He slid his tongue around her nipple, taking it into his mouth, and took pleasure from the way she moaned and moved beneath him, thrusting upward to meet his mouth, asking for more.

By the time he had her clothes off, he was so hard he thought he'd burst. She was wet and ready for him. She moved against his hand, hips thrusting. He fit her body against his. "Are you sure?"

Her response was to take hold of his buttocks and press him between her thighs. With one thrust, he found her, and the ecstasy of being inside Kara nearly made him come instantly.

"Derrick," she practically sobbed his name, rubbing against him like a wildcat too long without a mate. "God, you feel so good!"

"So do you. Kara, I can't hold back any longer."

"Then don't," she said, slipping her tongue into his mouth.

He wrapped his own tongue around hers, then

flowed into her, belatedly realizing he didn't have a condom…. Hadn't even thought about it.

It didn't matter. He loved her. He'd marry her in an instant, baby or no baby. Kara shuddered beneath him, crying out as she peaked. Slumping against her, their damp skin pressed together, Derrick lay his head on the pillow, near her shoulder, breathing in her scent.

"God, Kara."

"Yeah."

The single word held more meaning than a hundred words. She rubbed her soft hands over his back, his biceps.

"Kara. I—"

The words *love you* stuck in his throat as the telephone rang.

Kara let it ring. "They'll call back," she said against his neck, kissing his heated skin, arousing him again.

Somewhere in his foggy mind, reality set in. *Connor.* What if it was him calling? Was something wrong? Did his son need him? He opened his mouth to tell Kara to answer, just in case.

And then the answering machine clicked on.

"Hi." A man's voice. "You've reached Evan and Kara's house. We're not home right now. You know the routine."

The beep sounded overly loud. It seemed to echo off the walls. Beneath him, Kara tensed.

"*Mi hija,* it's Danita. I couldn't sleep, and I thought you might still be up. Call me when you get a minute. I just can't stop thinking... Well, you know. The jerk's always on my mind, like it or not. Talk to you later."

Any desire Derrick had felt died. He rolled off of her, leaning on one elbow as he looked into her eyes. He could barely see her face in the dim light from outside.

"You still have Evan's voice on your answering machine?"

"Derrick, I—I couldn't bring myself to erase it."

He sat up, raking his hands through his hair.

"Couldn't you at least change the tape?" He didn't give her time to answer. "I'll tell you why you didn't. It's because you're still in love with the guy, and you always will be." He got up, thrusting his legs into his underwear, his jeans. He knew he was acting like a jerk, but he was having a hard time reining in the hurt.

"Derrick, wait." Kara stood, clutching the quilt around her. "You're getting the wrong idea."

Shirt in hand, he paused. He wasn't the only person in the room who was in pain.

"Look, I shouldn't have rushed you," he said. "I thought maybe I could help you get past what you felt...what you feel...for him."

Kara's lips trembled, and he could see tears in her

eyes. "I'm sorry," she said, as the tears spilled down her cheek. He ignored the urge to wipe them away.

"Don't be." Derrick shrugged into his shirt.

"Please don't go. We need to talk."

"There's nothing to talk about." He put on his boots and hat, wishing he could wind the clock back to just before he'd kissed her. "Go call Danita back."

"I can't just stop loving Evan." She raised her hand in a gesture of frustration. "I can't turn off my feelings like a light switch. Can't you understand that?"

"I understand just fine, Kara," he said. "Good night."

He was beginning to see how Connor would want to break Kerri's pickup window.

CHAPTER SIXTEEN

KARA WOKE UP feeling like hell. She'd slept all of three hours. The phone rang, and she groaned, didn't want to answer. But she also didn't want to hear Evan's voice this morning.

"Hello."

"Kara, honey, are you all right?" Liz asked. "You sound like you're sick."

"I'm fine. I just didn't sleep very well."

"I'm sorry to hear that. I was wondering if you'd like to go to church with me, if you're up to it. We could do lunch again afterward."

She closed her eyes, clamping a hand over them. Church. Repentance. "Sure, Liz, I'd love to. I'll pick you up in an hour."

Kara hung up, let Lady into the backyard, then showered and dressed in a breezy sundress and, on a whim, a matching hat.

Derrick was only the second man she'd ever been with in her life, though he couldn't have known that.

And what he also didn't know was that she'd fallen in love with him. She loved him, yet she still loved Evan.

What was she going to do?

At least she'd still been on the pill. Somehow, she hadn't been able to stop herself from taking them after Evan had been killed. It was a final act—a silly one—of defiance. Of not wanting to admit her life had changed forever and that she had no reason to be on birth control.

When she left to pick up Liz, Kara refused to so much as look across the street at Derrick's place. She hoped he hadn't been too hard on Connor.

A short time later, Kara sat in the church pew next to Liz and did her best to focus on the sermon, but her thoughts were a confused whirlwind. She was glad when she and Liz were finally seated at a table at the diner. This time, she'd chosen to wait in the crowded line. No way could she bring herself to eat at the Spur.

They ordered, and Kara struck up idle conversation with Liz. "I noticed you were pretty friendly with Myrna and Violet today."

Liz squirmed. "Well, it's not for me to judge them."

Kara nearly choked on her ice water.

"I know," Liz said with a small laugh. "That's what I was doing before. But Myrna actually phoned me after seeing me at the Silver Spur."

"Really? You didn't mention it."

"That's because at first I was embarrassed, since I'd been catty about her and Violet. Anyway, Myrna invited me to go antiquing with her. She found this amazing shop over in Clear Water, and we had a ball together. Turns out we have a lot more in common than I thought."

"That's great." Kara couldn't remember hearing Liz sound this happy in a long while.

"So, did you go anywhere last night?" Liz asked.

Kara felt her entire body flush. She'd gone somewhere all right.

"Kara?"

"What? Oh—yes, I did. I, um, went to the Silver Spur."

"With your girlfriends?"

She sighed. "No. I went with Derrick and his son, which was a huge mistake."

"Why? What happened?" Liz asked casually, and Kara stared at her mother-in-law, taken aback by her lack of disapproval.

"You're right. I should've listened to my instincts. It's too soon for me to move on with another man when I still love Evan."

Liz reached out and took Kara's hand. "Kara. I didn't invite you out today just to have lunch and share church services."

"What do you mean?"

"I thought we could talk. Maybe go for a drive?"

"Sure." Kara frowned. "Is something wrong?"

"Yes and no. I'm fine, if that's what you mean." She turned her attention to the bowl of soup their waitress had placed in front of her. "I have something I want to speak to you about, that's all."

"Now you've got me curious."

"Well, it'll have to wait." Liz dipped her spoon into the broth. "There are too many ears in here." With a jerk of her head, she indicated the crowded room.

Kara could barely contain her curiosity, and was glad when the check came and they could leave.

Liz drove toward the cemetery, and Kara assumed they were going to visit Evan's grave, as they often did after Sunday services. But instead, Liz pulled in to a section of the cemetery where she and Bill owned joint plots. They'd been so sure they would pass on before their son, that they'd never thought to buy a family plot. Evan rested in an area several sections away.

Normally, she and Liz visited Evan's grave first, then Bill's. Kara really didn't think much about the reverse order. Maybe Liz needed to pay her respects to her husband right away this afternoon. Kara stood with her mother-in-law beside the black marble headstone that closely matched Evan's. It bore a picture of Bill, wearing a hat decorated with fishing lures, smiling as he held up a huge trout he'd caught at his favorite fishing hole. It was the way Kara remembered him best.

Liz had brought folding lawn chairs, and Kara helped her set them up near the gravestone. They sipped Cokes, and Liz put a white rose at the foot of the stone. "I brought you here for a reason," Liz said, sitting back down in her chair.

"Oh?"

"I had a dream last night. About me and Bill." Her eyes misted over. "It seemed so real, I woke up really devastated to find out it wasn't."

"I know what you mean," Kara said softly. "I dream about Evan all the time."

"This dream was different, somehow," Liz said. "It was like Bill was right there with me. And it made me remember all the more how happy I'd been with him."

Kara smiled. "He was a good man. I really miss him."

"You and me both." Liz pulled a tissue from her purse and dabbed at her eyes. "I don't think I'll ever stop crying for him. But Myrna said something to me the other day, when we were out, that got me thinking. She made the comment that she'd never expected to see me at the Silver Spur. You can imagine I was a bit startled by the irony of that."

"Is that what made you realize you'd misjudged her?" Kara asked.

"Partly. She told me it wasn't so much seeing me

in a bar as it was seeing me out having a good time." Liz raised her face to the sun. "I didn't even realize how much fun I'd actually had with you and your friends until I went home that night."

"You mean the rowdy, heathen crowd wasn't too much for you?"

"Okay, maybe I'm not one to drink. But the music was good, even if it was too loud. Kara, the bottom line is, I've been in denial. I didn't *want* to admit that I'd had fun because it made me feel guilty."

Kara stared at her, sure her ears were playing tricks on her. "I can relate."

"I'm sure you can. Myrna got me started thinking about things, and then when I dreamed about Bill last night, I finally realized something."

"What's that?"

"I was so happy with him, that all I've noticed since he's been gone is how sad I am without him. I've let the years pass without truly enjoying them, especially after I lost Evan, too."

"I know," Kara said, laying her hand on Liz's arm. "It's okay if you want to cry."

"No, sweetie, you don't understand." Liz crumpled the tissue in both hands. "I'm through with crying, and I'm through with being sad all the time. I'll never forget the years I had with Bill, or any of the memories we shared. But I've been so busy mourning, I forgot to live. And Bill wouldn't have wanted that."

Kara smiled sadly. "No, he wouldn't."

"And Evan wouldn't want that for you, either." She looked at her hands, clasped in her lap. "I'm so ashamed of myself, Kara. I've been too busy focusing on how I felt, on how much I needed you, to see that you might need someone to lean on, too. How selfish can a person be?"

"Don't say that," Kara said. "You're not selfish."

"I'm not? Do you realize that I sometimes leave the sprinkler on longer than necessary, hoping the grass will grow faster so you'll have to come over and mow it."

Kara laughed. "You do not."

"Oh, yes. And even though at first I really did need you to drive me around, and make sure I remembered to take my medication, et cetera, et cetera, I think I was actually scared. You're like a daughter to me, Kara, and I guess I was afraid of losing you, too."

"Oh, Liz. Why did you think that?"

Liz leveled her chin. "I figured if you met another man and fell in love, you'd marry him and move on with a new life…a new family. And I'd die alone and lonely. A dried up old hag, living with my ten cats."

Kara laughed. "You only have three cats. And I would never, ever forget about you." She leaned close, looking directly into Liz's eyes. "You're family, Liz. Now and forever. Nothing will ever change that."

"Oh, Kara." Liz leaned over, hugging her. "I'm so sorry. I don't know what I was thinking, trying to hold you back from finding happiness again."

"You weren't," Kara said. "I—I didn't think I was ready to move on, either."

"Until you met Derrick," Liz finished. "Am I right?"

"Is it that obvious?"

"Honey, I saw the way you looked at him that day we ate lunch at the Silver Spur. And more importantly, I saw the way he looked at you."

Kara's mood plummeted. "Maybe before. But after last night…"

"What happened last night?" Liz asked, then hastily added, "Never mind. It's none of my business."

"No. It's okay," Kara said. "As I said, I went out with Derrick and his son last night, to the Silver Spur." She explained about the incident with Kerri and her brat pack. Leaving out the intimate details, she simply ended with telling Liz how Derrick had come in when he dropped her off. "We were talking, and the phone rang. I let the machine get it, and…"

"Oh, God." Liz closed her eyes. "He heard Evan's voice."

Kara nodded. "It upset him pretty badly."

"I can imagine." Liz pursed her lips together in a hesitant gesture.

"What?"

"I didn't want to say anything," Liz said. "But, Kara, the message on the machine bothers me, too."

"What?" She would never have expected her mother-in-law to say such a thing.

"You know I love watching home videos of Evan, all the way from his first steps to your wedding day. And I'll always keep pictures of him out where I can see them every day. But, honey, when I call your house and get the machine…well, it makes me cry every time."

"Oh, Liz." Kara put a hand to her mouth. "I'm so sorry. I never thought…"

"Of course you didn't." Liz laid her hand on Kara's knee. " I don't ever want to forget what he sounded like…especially his laugh." Her eyes welled again, and she blinked. "But when I hear him on the machine, it reminds me every single time that he's *not* home. And he never will be."

Kara felt tears sliding down her own cheeks. "I'm so sorry," she said again. "I never thought about it that way. I just couldn't bring myself to change the message."

"I understand, Kara. Really, I do."

"I wish you'd said something."

"I didn't want to hurt you, dear. You've been hurt enough already…. Kara, don't let Derrick get away. He seems like a pretty good guy. Maybe you ought to give things a chance with him."

Kara twisted the plastic ring on her Coke bottle. "I don't know if I can."

"Of course you can," Liz said. "I was wrong to tell you it's too soon. That's not for me to decide, and it's certainly not anyone else's business in this town. If you want to go out with Derrick, then do it."

"Thank you," Kara said. "That means a lot to me. But I'm so confused right now. I care a lot about Derrick…I think I might even be falling in love with him."

"Then tell him."

Kara knew how hard those words had come. "I don't know if I'm ready."

"Well, your heart will tell you when you are." Liz looked at Bill's headstone. "I didn't think I'd ever fall in love again after Bill died. And I'm still not so sure I will. But I'm finally open to the idea." Her eyes sparkled. "And I really think you should keep going to the Silver Spur."

"It's a nice bar," Kara said, deadpan. "The music is good."

"And the guitar player is hot," Liz said, elbowing her.

Kara laughed. "Yeah. He is."

WHEN DERRICK and Connor pulled up in Shelly's driveway, she was outside, trimming the flower bed. She wore jean shorts and a black tank top, and her dark hair was pulled up into some sort of clamp thingy on the back of her head. She looked up, then turned off the Weed Eater and propped it against the porch.

"Hey, Connor," she said, coming over to the truck. "How was your visit with your dad?"

Derrick hated it that she always referred to Connor's time with him as a "visit," as though his son were a guest in his home.

"Fine," Connor said.

Shelly immediately picked up on his tone. "What is it?" Her gaze darted to Derrick. "Something happened, didn't it?"

He'd gone to get Connor's chair, and as his son settled into it, Derrick faced her. "Yes, Shelly, something happened." He looked at Connor. "Do you want to tell her or should I?"

Connor shrugged, not looking up. "I did something stupid."

Shelly folded her arms.

"I busted out Kerri Hendricks's truck window."

"You—Connor! Why on earth would you do something like that?" She glared at Derrick, as though blaming him. "Come inside and tell me what happened. You, too, Derrick."

He hated going into her house. But she was Connor's mother after all, and this was Connor's home…his second home as far as Derrick was concerned.

"Is Carl in?" he asked, stepping into the living room. Her husband was a truck driver.

"No. He's in Boise."

Shelly closed the door, keeping the swamp-cooler-chilled air from drifting outside. The room was somewhat dark, the brown area rug and closed drapes creating a cave-like atmosphere that was comforting and stifling at the same time.

"Have a seat," Shelly said.

He didn't want to, but he sat and listened while Connor told her what he'd done. Derrick filled in details here and there.

"I didn't know you'd made a habit of taking him to the Silver Spur," Shelly said.

"It was family night," Derrick explained. "There's no alcohol served."

To his surprise, she only nodded. "So, what are you planning to do about this, Connor? You're paying for the window, how?"

"Extra chores from Dad...my allowance from you." He shrugged. "I don't know."

"Well, I do," she said. "You're going to sell your laptop."

"What?" Connor's gaze shot up to meet hers. "Mom—no! You can't make me do that."

"Yes, I can."

"But it's the only thing I have to do around here!" He looked to Derrick for support. "Dad, tell her. If

I can't get online or play my video games, what am I supposed to do?"

Derrick opened his mouth, then clamped it shut. Shelly was right. Connor had been abusing his computer privileges lately anyway. He could always earn back the rights to another one down the line.

"I'm sure you'll find something," Shelly said firmly. "Aren't you taking riding lessons?"

"Well, yeah, but only once a week! What am I supposed to do the rest of the time?"

She shrugged. "Not my problem. I didn't throw the rocks."

"Damn!"

"That's another added chore," she said. "You know the rules."

"Mom!" Connor slumped in his chair as though his life were over. "This isn't fair!"

"Really?" Derrick gave him a stern look. "I'd say it wasn't fair of you to break Kerri's window, no matter what she did to you. We've already discussed this."

"Jeez." Connor stared at his hands in his lap, flexing them in nervous anger.

"It's not like you can't save up to buy another laptop," Shelly said, echoing Derrick's thoughts.

"That'll take forever."

"You can't expect Kerri to wait forever while you earn the money to pay for her window." Shelly smiled humorlessly. "I've seen her pickup. Etched glass doesn't come cheap."

"Her dad's loaded," Connor said. "He can get her a new window, then I'll pay him back."

"No," Derrick said. "You heard your mother. Your actions—your consequences."

"Sh—shoot!" Connor slammed back against his chair. "This sucks."

"It's settled," Shelly said. "Now go unpack your things."

Still grumbling, Connor made his way to his bedroom, his duffel bag hooked over the back of his chair.

Derrick waited until he was out of earshot. "Thanks," he said.

"For what?"

"For backing me on this. For thinking of a better punishment than I could." At least they were able to act as a team when it came to raising their son.

"What did you have in mind for punishing him?" Shelly asked.

He shrugged. "I'd only thought about the chore thing—and possibly grounding him from riding, but I didn't want to do that."

"No, and I'm glad you didn't." Shelly's expression softened. "I appreciate what you've done for him with that." She smiled. "He told me all about it on the phone. I've never seen him so excited."

"I know. I think it'll definitely be a good thing."

"When does he start his lessons? I'd like to come see him ride."

"Anytime now. Melanie got the medical forms back from Dr. Sorenson the other day, so everything's set."

"Well, if you want to start him riding while he's here with me, that would be fine," Shelly said. "I'll drive him to God's Little Acre, and you can come out, too."

"Sure." Her generosity took him by surprise. Normally, she was a stickler on not giving him any extra time with Connor, other than for special occasions like Father's Day or a birthday.

"All right, then." Shelly stood. "I'll be in touch."

"Fair enough." Derrick turned to go out the door.

"Derrick."

He turned. "Yeah?"

She hesitated. "Maybe we could work something out for you to spend more time with Connor during the school year. Maybe even joint custody."

He stared at her. "You're serious?"

She nodded. "He's told me he wants to be with you more, and he's getting older now. He needs his father."

Derrick smiled, turning back to give her a brief hug. "Thank you, Shelly."

"You're welcome."

"And one more thing."

"What's that?" she asked.

"Thanks for letting him buy that pawnshop guitar. He really surprised me."

She chuckled. "That's exactly what he wanted to do. I'm proud of him."

"So am I." He paused with his hand on the doorknob. "I guess if we didn't do a lot of things right in the past, at least we got one thing right."

He opened the door. "See you later."

As he made his way to the truck, he began to think about Kara again, and the dark mood that had kept him company all week returned. What was he going to do about his feelings for her?

He couldn't very well just turn them off. Yet he couldn't keep letting her hurt him, hanging on to Evan's memory and everything she'd shared with the guy. Not that he'd ever expect her to forget her husband. He simply wanted her to let go.

CHAPTER SEVENTEEN

KARA PICKED THE PHONE UP twice before she actually got the nerve to dial Derrick's number.

Derrick didn't answer right away, and she nearly hung up. It was Friday. Maybe he'd already left for the Spur.

"Hello?"

"Hi, Derrick. Did I catch you at a bad time?"

"Kara—no, uh, I'm just getting off the other line with my mother. Can you hold?"

"Why don't you call me back when you're done?"

"No, really, we were just about to say goodbye. Hang on."

That he was talking to his mother did her heart some good. She wondered if he'd made any progress with his dad.

"Kara? You still there?"

"I'm here."

He was silent a beat. "How are you?"

"Doing okay. Listen, Derrick, I don't like the way things ended between us the last time you were here." She plunged on before she could lose her nerve. "I was wondering if you'd like to go horse-back riding with me tomorrow, and maybe have a picnic."

He laughed. "I'd thought about asking you on a picnic."

"But, we won't actually be eating on horseback," Kara quipped, trying to hide her nervous anticipation. "That could get a bit bumpy."

His laugh warmed her. "I'd say. What do you want me to bring?"

"Nothing. I've got it."

"You sure?"

"Uh-huh. Just meet me at the stable, say about eight-thirty, if that's not too early? That'll give us time to ride first."

"That's fine," Derrick said.

"See you tomorrow, then."

She hung up, then dialed Danita's number.

"Hey, girl," Danita said. "What's up?"

"Hopefully, my nerve."

"Aha. This has something to do with Derrick I assume?"

"How'd you guess?" Kara sighed. "You're right, I need to move on, one way or another. I'm still not sure I'm ready for a relationship, but I also can't string Derrick along."

"Makes sense to me, and for the record, *mi hija,*

I think you've been doing a pretty fine job of getting on with your life."

"Thank you." Her friend's praise meant so much to Kara. "I've invited Derrick on a horseback ride and picnic tomorrow morning. I borrowed one of Ray and Sharon's horses last time I took him on a ride, but I hate to make a habit of asking."

"So you're asking to borrow my horse instead." Danita laughed. "Say no more. I'd be happy to contribute to the cause."

"What cause is that?" Kara asked, dryly.

"Hooking you up with Derrick, of course. He's perfect for you, *mi hija*."

"I hope so." If any man was, he was. If not...

"You know I wouldn't loan Choctaw to just anyone," Danita said.

"I know. I promise I'll look after him like he's my own. And I already know that Derrick's a good rider with light hands."

"Good. I'm not surprised, the way he plays that guitar...like he's making love to it." Danita gave an exaggerated sigh. "Have you slept with him yet?"

"Danita!"

"Well, have you? Come on, Kara, I have to live vicariously through you, now that I'm not getting any."

"You could change that, you know." She hesitated. "Once. But I blew it."

"What do you mean?"

"I'll tell you all about it when I see you." *Well, most of it anyway.*

"Hey, how about over a couple of beers? Want to meet me at the Silver Spur?"

"I'd rather wait until tomorrow night, if you don't mind."

"Say no more. Tomorrow it is. That way you can fill me in *and* see your cowboy."

Kara laughed. "Want to meet me at the stable in the morning with your saddle and stuff, or did you leave it in the tack room last time?"

"I did. Sharon finally put a lock on the door."

"Good. I'm getting sick of lugging my saddle home."

"I'll tell Sharon you're using mine. See you tomorrow."

"Thanks, Danita. Bye."

Kara hung up, her stomach high on anticipation. If all went well with Derrick tomorrow, then she'd have plenty to celebrate at the Silver Spur.

Otherwise, she'd never set foot in the place again.

DERRICK RODE BESIDE Kara on Danita's tricolored overo Paint, wishing he could preserve this moment in time. The air was cool and crisp, a breeze blowing across the peaks of the surrounding mountains. The graceful arc of the trees over the trail made a quiet canopy that soothed his nerves. He wasn't sure what had caused Kara's abrupt change in attitude, but he wasn't about to look a gift horse in the mouth—pun intended. He'd missed her.

"This gelding is something," he said, reaching down to stroke Choctaw's neck. The horse was big, about a hand taller than Kara's mare.

"Isn't he? I love him."

"It was nice of Danita to let me ride him."

"She's a great friend."

He kept up the small talk as they rode, still curious as to why Kara had invited him on the ride. By eleven o'clock, they'd veered off the trail and ridden through the trees into a clearing. A creek wound alongside it, the water whispering over the rocks. The perfect spot.

"How's this look?" Kara asked. "You ready to eat?"

"Fine by me. I'm starving."

Kara looked so beautiful this morning, her cheeks flushed from the gallop they'd taken a short time ago, her long hair hanging down her back beneath the straw cowboy hat she wore. And her sexy curves filled out the jeans and tank top she wore just right.

God he wanted her.

Derrick swung off Choctaw's back as they halted the horses beneath some shade trees. They'd brought lead ropes, having left the horses' halters on beneath their bridles, and now tied them to a tree.

Kara took her saddlebags off her horse and laid

them on a blanket she'd unfurled. Derrick helped her get out the sandwiches, pop and plastic containers of potato salad and chocolate cake.

"This looks good," he said as they sat down near the edge of the creek. "Did you make that cake?"

"Oh, yes. I made it from scratch, and I even grew the wheat for the flour and raised the chickens for the eggs. So I hope you appreciate it."

He chuckled. "Absolutely."

She smiled at him, and he felt as melted as the fudge frosting on the cake. Once they'd finished eating, Derrick put the containers back into the saddlebags, then sat close to Kara, sipping his pop.

"I have a confession to make," Kara said.

"What's that?"

"I had a reason for inviting you out here today."

He tensed. "Yeah?"

She nodded. "Derrick, I really am sorry about what happened the other night."

"Kara, we don't have to rehash all that."

"I put a new message on my answering machine."

Her gaze held his, and Derrick's hope soared. "You shouldn't have erased it. It wasn't my intention—"

"I didn't. I kept the tape. But I should've changed it sooner." She laughed without humor. "Even my mother-in-law told me it upset her, hearing Evan's voice on there. I didn't mean to hurt anyone."

"Of course you didn't." He reached out and took her hand. "I'm sorry I got so bent out of shape."

"I can't blame you," Kara said. "If the shoe were on the other foot, I would've gotten upset, too."

He hesitated. "I only got upset because I'm a jealous fool." *Jealous of a dead man.* He leaned forward and kissed her.

Kara kissed him back, softly at first, then more aggressively. It was with the greatest effort that Derrick pulled away.

He held Kara by the shoulders, looking straight into her eyes. "If we don't slow down, I'm going to tear your clothes off," he said. "And I can't do that unless I know you're really ready for this, Kara." Just because she'd taken Evan's voice off her machine didn't mean anything had changed.

She took a deep breath and let it out. "You're right. I brought you out here so we could talk."

Reluctantly, he lowered his hands to his lap. "I'm listening."

"I had lunch with my mother-in-law the other day, and she got me thinking. What she said to me made me realize—"

Derrick's cell phone rang, cutting through the peacefulness of the surrounding mountains like a blaring horn in traffic. "I'm sorry," he said, taking the phone from his shirt pocket. He looked at the display. Shelly's number.

"Connor?"

"No, Derrick it's me." The tone of her voice alarmed him. She rarely called his cell.

"What's wrong?"

"Connor's missing." He could tell she was trying not to cry, not to panic.

"Missing? What happened?"

"I—I took him out to the riding center. He said he wanted to see his friend, Lisa. He promised they'd only ride in the arena, so I left him there and now they're both gone!"

"Where's Melanie?"

"She wasn't home. There were just a couple of stable hands, working in the barn."

"The kids aren't allowed to ride unless Melanie and her assistants are there!"

"I didn't know that," Shelly wailed. "Connor said Lisa had her own horse and—never mind, Derrick, just hurry and get here! Melanie's forming a search party. They think the kids took off riding on the trails!"

"I'll be right there." He snapped the phone shut.

"Connor's missing?" Kara stood and hastily rolled up the picnic blanket.

"He and Lisa took off on horseback. Melanie's gathering a search party."

"I know a shortcut to her ranch."

He untied Choctaw's lead rope. "Let's go."

THE SHORTCUT TOOK THEM to God's Little Acre as the crow flies, cutting off three of the five miles they would've otherwise had to travel, and Kara rode the entire distance with her heart in her throat.

By the time they arrived, people were already gathered on horseback, Melanie's Arabian saddled and tied to the hitching post.

"Derrick, I am so, *so* sorry," Melanie said. "One of my volunteers saw the kids take off, but she got distracted by a client who pulled into the driveway, and—"

"Let's just find them."

"I've already got riders out looking, and as you can see, more people keep showing up."

"Which direction did they go?" Kara asked.

"When Stephanie saw them, it looked like they were headed for the trail that leads to Cutback Mountain." Melanie gestured toward the distant peak. "But there are several ways in."

"I'm familiar with the area," Kara said.

"Me, too," Derrick said. "I've taken Connor fishing there."

"Do you know about the shortcut through Piney Creek?" Melanie asked.

Kara nodded. "I was just about to mention it."

"Then you and Derrick take the shortcut, and I'll take a group and branch out over some of the other trails. If anyone finds the kids, they'll fire a signal—

two shots, followed by three more." Melanie shaded her eyes against the sun. "I don't suppose either of you have a pistol?"

Derrick shook his head.

"Hang on."

She hurried to speak to a tall, lanky cowboy, saddling a horse tied to a trailer. The guy nodded, then reached into his saddlebag and pulled out a holstered revolver.

Melanie came back with it. "Here." She held it out to Derrick. "You can borrow Chuck's. He's got another."

"Put it in Kara's saddlebags," he directed her. "That okay with you?"

"Of course," Kara said.

With a hasty farewell, they were off.

"It's a beautiful ride to the lake by Cutback Mountain," Kara said. "I'll bet that's where Connor and Lisa have gone."

"I hope so." Derrick's expression belied his calm words.

Kara prayed the kids were safe, and that someone would find them, wherever they might've ridden.

CONNOR'S BACK ACHED from above his waist all the way up between his shoulder blades, and his arm muscles were getting tired, but he didn't care. Being with Lisa—just the two of them on horseback—was worth it. And worth the punishment he'd face if his dad found out he'd tricked his mom into taking him to God's Little Acre.

So long as he and Lisa got back before Melanie came home, they ought to be okay. They'd initially meant only to take turns riding Maverick in the arena, but then Lisa had thought it would be all right to ride Lollipop, and before he knew it, Connor had talked her into taking a trail ride—just a short one. That short ride had turned longer than they'd planned, but as they approached the shortcut to Cutback Mountain, Lisa smiled, making him forget everything else.

"You're going to love the lake," she said. "It's beautiful."

"I'll bet." He didn't want to spoil her surprise by telling her his dad had taken him fishing there before.

The shortcut trail was steep and narrow, and Connor began to sweat as the horses climbed. He clutched Lollipop's saddle, grateful for the gear that kept him steady on the horse's back, and even more thankful for the gelding's quiet nature and surefootedness. He looked down to his left and realized the ravine wasn't as steep as he'd feared. But the drop was still a good ten to twelve feet, and Connor was relieved when the trail led to firmer footing again, and the lake came into view.

"There it is," Lisa said. "Isn't it gorgeous?"

Not as gorgeous as you.

"Yeah, it's awesome."

They trotted the horses across the clearing and halted at the water's edge. A pile of driftwood, butted up against a fallen log, formed a haphazard stack, an ideal place for Lisa to dismount. She'd tied her crutches to her saddle, while Connor carried her braces on his. Leaning on Maverick for support, Lisa now got them, then tethered the horse to the log.

"Come on." She motioned to Connor. "I'll hold Lollipop parallel with the log and help you down."

"I don't know." He eyed the pile of driftwood. It seemed a long way from the saddle to the log.

"It's not as far down as it looks," Lisa said. "Trust me. Just grab the hand grip and I'll help you."

"All right." He didn't want Lisa to think he was a wuss.

Getting off the horse turned out not to be as awkward as Connor had thought, and before he knew it, he was sitting beside Lisa on the log, his back propped against the driftwood for support.

"Man, this is awesome!" The only sounds were the soft slapping of waves against the water's edge, and the chatter of birds in the nearby trees.

"Isn't it?" Lisa beamed at him. "I knew you'd love it."

Connor could barely take his eyes off her. She'd removed her riding helmet, as had he, and her dark hair hung loose down her back. He wanted to touch it. It was nearly to her waist. He loved long hair on a girl.

Discreetly, using his arms for leverage, he scooted a little closer.

"So, what's it like going to private school?" he asked, his nerves humming at Lisa's nearness. He could smell the sweet, green-apple scent of her shampoo. She tucked her hair behind one ear, revealing two tiny, silver studs and a horseshoe-shaped earring in her lobe.

"It's pretty good," she said. "Since everybody there is physically challenged, it basically puts us all on an even keel. Nobody makes fun of anybody else, well, at least for the most part." She shrugged. "Even handicapped people can be jerks sometimes."

He laughed. "Yeah, but I'll bet you don't have to put up with as much sh—crap as I do, going to Sage Middle School. I can't *wait* to move on to high school this fall," he added dryly. "With old Fart-Bart and his bunch."

"Don't let them bother you," Lisa said. "They're losers." She grinned. "I'm sort of glad you busted Kerri's window. She thinks she's all that. She was always snotty to me, and my older sister—same grade as her—even before I got hurt."

"How did you get hurt?"

"Barrel racing accident. My foot got hung up in the stirrup, and I was dragged." She frowned. "I had to learn to walk and ride all over again, and I couldn't keep my barrel horse. He was too much horse for me. That's why my parents got Maverick."

"Damn. You're pretty tough."

Lisa laughed. "So, why don't you go to West Creek?" she asked. "Won't your dad let you?"

"It's not that." A tiny green caterpillar inched its way across the log toward his knee. Connor held out his finger, let it crawl onto his knuckle, then lowered it gently to the grass. "He doesn't have the money for private school, and neither does my mom."

"Oh." She nudged him with her elbow. "Maybe that'll change when your dad becomes a famous singer."

He grinned. "I doubt that'll happen, even though I think he's good enough. Dad doesn't think he is, so he's never tried Nashville or anything."

"I think he's really good, too," Lisa said. "And so are you." She took his hand, and Connor's heart nearly leapt from his chest.

They sat like that, looking at each other, for a long moment. Connor swallowed. It was now or never. He leaned toward Lisa, and touched his lips to hers. She kissed him back, and it was the best thing that had ever happened to him. He'd closed his eyes, but now he snuck a peek. Hers were closed, so he shut his again. They traded a few awkward pecks, then

Connor drew back. He needed air. And he didn't want Lisa to feel how sweaty his palms were.

In a casual move, he let go of her hand and put his arm around her. "Got a boyfriend?" he asked, grinning.

"I do now," she said. She leaned toward him, and he got all set to kiss her again. But suddenly her eyes widened. "Oh, crap! Lollipop."

Connor jerked his head around, and saw the horse had tugged his reins loose from the log, and was now grazing a few feet away. "He'll be all right," he said. "He's just eating."

"No, he won't." Lisa squirmed out from under his arm, reaching for her crutches. "It's the one bad habit Lollipop has. He's the best horse Melanie owns, but he's harder than heck to catch if you don't have grain, unless he's in a pen or box stall." She started slowly toward the gelding, speaking softly to him.

Lollipop ignored her, head down, grazing away. But for every step Lisa took, he took two in the opposite direction, and pretty soon, he was moving away at a steady walk.

"Whoa, Lollipop," Lisa said. "Whoa, boy." She moved a little faster.

The gelding lifted his head, cast a look over his shoulder, then trotted away.

Maverick let out a whinny of protest, but the

chestnut kept going, faster and faster until he broke into a lope, then a gallop.

"Oh, hell!" Connor clamped both hands to his head.

"I'll go get him." As quickly as she could, Lisa got out of her leg braces, then climbed onto Maverick and set off after Lollipop.

But the chestnut gelding was already out of sight.

CHAPTER EIGHTEEN

KARA RODE BESIDE Derrick until they came to a point where the Piney Creek trail crossed a stream and narrowed as it went uphill. She dropped in behind him as they climbed, keeping an eye out for tracks.

"Look," Derrick said.

Kara leaned in the saddle to see past him. Fresh horse manure lay scattered on the trail, tiny gnats buzzing all around.

"That's got to be from one of their horses," Derrick said. "It looks like a couple of riders passed this way." He indicated hoof prints in the dirt.

"Probably." Or it could be some search riders had passed by here, or any horseback riders, but Kara didn't want to douse Derrick's hope.

A few minutes later, the trail widened as it leveled out. To their left lay a ravine; to the right, the mountain sloped gradually downward to meet a small clearing. And across that clearing trotted Lollipop.

Kara's heart leaped into her throat. "Oh, God!"

Derrick had been focused on guiding Choctaw over a fallen log, but at Kara's words he looked up.

"Connor!" He nudged Choctaw with his boot heels, hustling the Paint over the log. The gelding's hooves clipped the wood as he jumped forward. "Connor!" Derrick shouted louder.

"Take it easy, Derrick. You're spooking your horse."

The words were barely out, when Choctaw side-stepped—too close to the ravine's edge. Derrick moved to correct him, but the gelding's hooves slipped, then slid out from under him as the dirt and rock gave way.

"Derrick!" Kara urged Indio forward, making a grab for Choctaw's bridle. But her fingers closed on air, and she swallowed a scream as the horse fell backward, rolling and sliding down the side of the mountain like an errant tumbleweed.

"Oh, Lord!" Kara swung from the saddle.

She stood, helpless, staring down at Derrick. He'd been thrown as Choctaw fell, and the gelding now rolled past and nearly over him, kicking and thrashing in an effort to regain his footing. The ground dropped at a steep angle for about twelve feet, then leveled out at an old line shack.

Leafy shrubs partially covered the dilapidated building, and Choctaw tumbled and slammed through them into the weathered, board wall. He lashed out with both rear hooves, striking it with a solid thump, then scrambled to his feet.

Derrick staggered to his feet as well. "Whoa!" He weaved toward the frightened horse.

"Derrick, stand back!" Kara shouted. "He'll run over you!" She started down the hillside, clutching Indio's reins.

And then she heard it—an angry, swarming sound. Wasps—yellow jackets—poured out from under the eaves of the line shack, where a paperlike nest hung. Exacting revenge, the wasps swarmed the horse, and Choctaw took off, bucking and snorting.

Kara pressed against Indio as the gelding lunged back up the mountain, nearly plowing Kara down. In the chaos, she'd forgotten all about Lollipop, trotting their way. Now the two horses joined up and took off hell-bent for leather down the trail toward the stables. Indio struggled to join them, letting out a loud whinny.

"Easy," Kara soothed, gripping the reins firmly. "Whoa!"

Her gaze shot to Derrick. He'd taken off his hat and was swatting frantically at the wasps, at the same time trying to run from them.

"Derrick, don't smash them!" Kara shouted. Wasps emitted a chemical alarm pheromone when crushed, signaling fellow wasps to come sting anything and anyone within reach.

"Damn it!" He swung his hat.

Too late.

Kara stood, frozen, as Derrick ran, bellowing. He started up the hillside. They'd passed a stream. Was it deep enough for cover? Kara turned reflexively, and saw Lisa riding up the trail on Maverick.

"Lisa, stay back!" Kara shouted.

A wasp landed on her shoulder and she flinched, trying not to panic. Indio snorted and shook her head as wasps buzzed around her. The mare yanked the reins from her grasp, and Kara grabbed the saddlebags just as Indio took off. She felt the sharp pain of a sting.

"Turn back!" Kara shouted. Lisa halted in confusion. "Go!" Kara waved one arm, then fumbled for the pistol inside the saddlebags.

By now Derrick had managed to stagger up the hill to the trail. Kara gasped when she saw him. Hives had broken out all over his face and the backs of his hands. Yellow jackets danced around him, dodging the cowboy hat he continued to swing fruitlessly. His breathing was labored, and he began to cough.

"Kara, get help!" He choked out the words, voice hoarse, then dropped to his knees and threw up.

Kara pulled out the pistol, aimed it down the mountain at a tree stump near the line shack and fired.

CONNOR SNAPPED HIS HEAD around at the sound of gunshots, echoing through the valley. Two, then three more. *What the hell?*

"Lisa!" he called, his heart slamming against his ribs. He'd never felt so helpless, sitting like the proverbial bump on the damned fallen log, unable to do anything. Why the hell had he been so stupid to ride out here? "Lisa!"

Dear God, had someone shot at her? Maybe a hunter had mistaken Lollipop for a deer or an elk. But it wasn't hunting season. Connor's mouth went dry as he stared into the distance. "Lisa!" he screamed.

The silence reverberated around him, and the minutes stretched like hours. It seemed forever before he finally heard hoof beats coming his way. But it wasn't Lisa. It was Melanie and one of her volunteers—George—riding along, leading Lollipop.

"Connor, are you all right?" Melanie called, urging her horse into a lope.

"Where's Lisa?"

"She's back at the riding center," George said.

"What the heck's going on?" He didn't like the looks on their faces. "Is she hurt? Did Maverick throw her?"

"It's not Lisa," Melanie said quietly. "It's your dad."

Connor's heart all but stopped. "What do you mean? W-was there an accident?"

"Yellow jackets," George said, getting down off his horse. "Your dad and Kara were out looking for you kids, and they ran into a nest of 'em. Looks like your dad's allergic." He offered Connor a hand.

"The helicopter's on it's way," Melanie said.

"On it's way where?" Connor's throat closed. And then he heard it—the sound of a chopper in the distance.

Shit. Oh shit, this was all his fault. If his dad hadn't come looking for him…

"Come on," George said, slipping an arm around Connor's shoulders. Taking hold of his belt, the old cowboy hefted him to his feet, then swung him up into Lollipop's saddle. "You okay to ride?"

"Yeah. Let's go."

Every muscle in his upper body felt like wet spaghetti, but Connor gritted his teeth.

Now he knew how his dad felt.

If anything happened to him, Connor would never forgive himself.

KARA LAY ON A GURNEY in the emergency room, staring down the nurse who'd made her put on a hospital gown. "I'm fine," she said for the hundredth time. "I want to see Derrick!"

"Kara, please sit back." The nurse—her nametag read *Marge*—pressed her gently against the pillow as Kara struggled to get up. "We need to make sure you aren't going to have an allergic reaction of your own. Derrick's in good hands with Dr. Erickson, I promise."

Tears burned Kara's eyes and spilled down her face as she flopped back against the pillow, angry, frustrated…and terrified. Derrick had looked so still, so…near death, as the medics loaded him into the helicopter. They'd taken her, too, but the entire flight was a blur.

"Listen to the nurse," Beth said firmly. She'd been out with the search party, and had rushed to the hospital with Danita and Hannah. "You've got to take care of yourself, otherwise you won't be of help to anyone."

Danita stood at the foot of the gurney. "Kara, calm down, *mi hija,*" she soothed, a worried frown creasing her forehead. "Beth's right. We have to take care of you, too." She moved forward to take Kara's hand once the nurse left the room.

"What am I going to do?" Kara stared into her best friend's eyes. "He can't die, Danita. He just can't!"

"Shhh," Hannah said. "Don't even think it!"

"Derrick's made of tougher stuff than that." Danita rubbed her shoulder. "I promise."

"That's right." Beth nodded vehemently. "It'll take more than a few bees to knock him down."

"They were wasps," Kara said. "And he's allergic! Damn, I didn't know—he didn't even know, apparently." Her mind raced. "Where's Connor?"

"He's fine," Danita said. "He's in the waiting

room with his mom and Melanie. And I called Liz—she's on her way over."

Knowing her friends, her family, had pulled together made Kara feel like crying all the more. What would she do without them?

Worse still, what would she do without Derrick?

She'd been so afraid to love him, so afraid to cheat on Evan's memory. And now, Kara realized she'd only cheated herself.

"I'm going to him." Kara shoved past her well-meaning friends, not caring that she wore only a flimsy hospital gown. Gripping the back of it closed, she rushed through the emergency room hall in her stocking feet.

"Miss, what are you doing—?" A nurse hurried toward her.

"I want to see Derrick Mertz," Kara said. "Now."

"Yes, ma'am. Follow me." The woman led Kara to another set of exam rooms. "He's in room three, but you'll have to wait out here," the nurse said. "The doctors are working on him." Her expression was sympathetic.

"Kara," Danita said softly behind her, laying her hand on Kara's shoulder.

Kara swung around. Behind Danita stood Beth, Hannah…and Liz.

"Oh, Liz!" Kara reached out to her mother-in-law. "I can't do this again. I can't!"

"I know," Liz said, folding her into a hug. "It's going to be all right, Kara."

Hurting in a way she'd thought she'd never hurt again, Kara let Liz guide her to a nearby chair.

"Pull yourself together," Liz said. "For Connor's sake. You're going to scare him if he sees you this way."

Kara nodded. "I need to get dressed."

"But the nurse..." Beth started. "Oh, what the hell. Come on."

She helped Kara to her feet, and hustled her back the way they'd came. Within minutes, Kara was dressed and in the waiting room, where Connor, pale as ice, sat beside his mom with Kevin.

"Kara." He wheeled toward her as Shelly rose to her feet. "Where's my dad? How is he?"

"He's still with the doctors." Kara made a conscious effort to get hold of herself. She laid her hand on Connor's shoulder. "He'll be fine," she said, wishing she believed it.

"This is all my fault," Connor said. "Damn it, why did I have to be so stupid?"

"It's not your fault." Kara looked to Shelly for support.

"I told you that," Shelly said. "Connor, you've got to calm down, son."

"I can't calm down!" He turned on her, tears in his eyes. "My dad's going to die from some stupid wasp stings, and it's all because of me. Everything bad happens to him because of me. I wish I'd never been born!"

"Connor!" Shelly took a step back, hurt.

Even Kevin stared, openmouthed.

"Don't say that," Kara said, kneeling in front of Connor. "Look at me. Look at me, damn it!" Her blunt words got his attention. "Your dad loves you more than life itself. He would do anything for you, Connor. That's why he went out looking for you, and that's why you have to stay strong for him." Even as she spoke, she realized the truth in her words. "We all have to."

She gripped his hands and looked around—at Shelly and Kevin, at her friends—and then she saw a familiar woman walk into the room.

"Grandma!" Connor said. "You got here fast!"

"You'd better know it," Carolyn Mertz said.

"We were already on our way."

Kara looked at the tall, silver-haired cowboy behind Carolyn.

"Grandpa?" Connor's jaw dropped.

Shelly gasped. "Vernon!"

"Your grandpa finally had a change of heart," Carolyn said, a humorless laugh escaping her. "We were halfway here when you called my cell phone."

"How's your dad?" Vernon asked, his voice gruff, tight.

"I don't know." Connor looked young and scared, sitting there, gripping his grandmother's hand.

Kara couldn't stop staring at Derrick's father. He'd taken the first step.

She only hoped he wasn't too late.

CHAPTER NINETEEN

DERRICK WOKE UP with the sound of wasps buzzing in his head. His mouth was dry, and his head felt like he'd drank a quart of tequila and swallowed the worm to boot.

"Welcome back, Mr. Mertz. You gave us quite a scare."

He looked up into the smiling face of a nurse with short, dark hair. She checked his IV drip and took his blood pressure. His mind was fuzzy, but he remembered the wasps…Choctaw rearing…

"Where's Kara? Is she hurt?" His fuzzy brain began to function. "Where's my son?"

"He's fine—he keeps asking about you—and if Kara is the pretty young woman who came in on the helicopter with you, she's waiting anxiously. I'll get her." She unfastened the Velcro cuff and exited the room.

Helicopter? Hell. He had no memory of anything past trying to get back up the hillside to Kara.

A moment later, she came into the room. She looked tired.

He'd never been more glad to see her.

"You found Connor—he's okay?" Derrick asked. "What happened?"

"He's fine." Kara sat in the chair beside his bed, staring anxiously at him. "His horse just got away from him, that's all. He's waiting to see you."

"So he wasn't thrown?"

"No. Are you all right?"

"I'm fine. And Lisa's okay, too?"

"She sure is."

Derrick closed his eyes, sending up a silent prayer of thanks.

Kara moved to sit on the edge of his bed. She stroked his hair. "God, you scared me!" A tear squeezed out of the corner of her eye. "I thought you were going to die."

"That makes two of us," he said dryly. "I couldn't breathe."

She nodded. "They gave you epinephrine…. You didn't know you're allergic to wasp stings?"

He shook his head. "I've never been stung before. I always wear bug spray when I go fishing." He reached out and brushed the tears from her face. "Hey, no crying. I'm fine."

"Well, you scared the hell out of me," she said again.

"Is Danita's horse all right?"

"Amazingly enough, yes. Hannah checked him over. He got a couple of stings and a few scrapes, but that's it."

"God, I feel so stupid."

"Why? It could've happened to anyone. I'm just glad you're all right."

He took her hand and brought it to his mouth, pressing a kiss against her fingers. "Me, too. I'd hate to have missed out on seeing you look at me the way you're looking at me now. Remind me to thank those yellow jackets."

"That's not funny," Kara said. But she smiled.

He touched her cheek. Turning her chin, he examined a swollen area on her temple. "Looks like they got you, too."

"A little. But I'm fine—" she leaned into his touch, closing her hand over his wrist "—now that I know you're all right."

"So, where's Connor?"

"In the waiting room with Shelly and your mom, and half a dozen other people who are worried sick about you." Her eyes brightened. "As a matter of fact, there's somebody who's very anxious to see you. Hang on, I'll be right back."

Puzzled, Derrick waited. A moment later, he thought he was hallucinating when his dad walked through the door.

"Hello, son."

"Dad—what are you doing here?" *How long had he been unconscious?*

Vernon stood hesitantly at the foot of the bed. "I came to tell you how sorry I am for being such a stubborn old fool." Though his voice was gruff, he was looking at Derrick affectionately. Affection wasn't something Derrick had expected from his dad since he was a kid. "Your mom and I had decided to drive down this weekend and surprise you. We were on our way when Shelly called." He cleared his throat, and a long moment passed before he continued. "When I think that I might've been too late…"

"But you're not," said Derrick, gripped by the surrealism of this moment. "It's good to see you, Dad."

"It's good to see you, too, son." Vernon moved to the side of the bed and put his hand on Derrick's shoulder. "You'd better hurry up and get out of this damned hospital. We've got a lot of catching up to do."

Derrick gripped his dad's arm. It felt good to touch him. To breathe in the familiar scent of his cologne. Suddenly, he felt like a kid—the one who used to fish with his dad.

He cleared his throat. "Yeah, we do."

"We could go fishing," Vernon said, as though reading his thoughts. "It's been a long time."

"It has." Derrick looked straight at his father,

taking in the silver of his hair beneath his beat-up old Stetson. The lines on his face...

But he looked great.

Vernon grinned. "Just as long as you bring your bug spray."

Derrick laughed, and then his dad was pulling him into a hug.

"Damn it, I missed you son. I missed you so much." He clapped Derrick on the back, squeezed him so hard he could barely breathe.

"I missed you, too, Dad." Derrick no longer hid his tears. "Hell, what took us so long?"

Over Vernon's shoulder, Derrick saw his mom and Connor, standing in the doorway—Kara behind them.

And in that moment, he knew he had everything in his life a man could want.

He wasn't about to let any of it get away.

KARA WENT HOME from the hospital late that night, exhausted but happy. A sense of peacefulness filled her—something she hadn't felt since Evan's death. She went out to her backyard and sat with Lady, enjoying the quiet. She thanked God Derrick was fine. That he and his dad had had a change of heart, and that everything, for once, seemed right with her world and those around her.

"Are you watching, Evan?" Kara whispered, looking up at the stars. "Do you understand?"

Did he know she would always love him? But she couldn't deny herself Derrick's love and companionship any longer? Was Liz right? Would Evan want her to move on...to be happy?

Kara thought he would.

She went inside, and got a cardboard box from the back bedroom. She went through the house, a tightness in her throat, and packed up the last of Evan's things. His work boots...his hard hat...his jacket that hung beside it on a peg near the door. In a smaller box, she packed away their wedding photo. The last thing she started to put away was the picture on her nightstand.

Kara sat on the edge of the bed, staring at the framed photo. Evan smiled out at her, his expression full of humor, love. Evan was Evan, and Derrick was Derrick. One had nothing to do with the other, and there was room in her heart for more than one man.

"I love you, Evan. Always." Kara kissed the photograph, then carefully tucked it away inside her dresser drawer before returning to the packed box. When she taped it shut, her hands were shaking. But the closure made everything all right.

Kara stored the box in the garage, beside one that contained other mementos she couldn't yet part with. She'd give them to Liz. Soon.

She closed the garage door and went back inside the house.

That night, Kara didn't have any nightmares. And she woke up feeling like a new woman. One with a brighter future.

SIX DAYS AFTER he'd come home from the hospital, Derrick dressed in his favorite black, western shirt and a new pair of jeans. Tonight was going to change his life, one way or another. And he was as nervous as a long-tailed cat in a room full of rocking chairs.

"Hurry up, Dad!" Connor called. "We don't want to be late."

"Coming." Derrick checked his shirt pocket for the hundredth time, patting it for luck.

Family night at the Silver Spur was crowded as usual. He'd made arrangements to meet Kara there, rather than take her with him, using a made-up excuse about having to meet his band early. He didn't want anything to spoil the surprise, and if he drove her to the Spur himself, he'd never be able to hold back telling her what he had to say.

And he wanted to do it in front of all their friends. Hell, he wanted to shout his love for Kara to the world.

As he looked out over the crowded room, he saw her, sitting at the center table closest to the band—Tina had made sure to reserve it. Danita,

Beth and Hannah sat with her, as well as Connor and Lisa. Danita gave him a little wink, and Connor hid his hand beneath the table and gave the thumbs-up sign.

Cripes. Derrick hoped Kara wouldn't kill him for doing this in front of everyone. He stepped up to the microphone.

"Good evening. How are ya'll doing tonight?"

The crowd cheered and whistled.

"All right. Well, we're here to have some fun, so let's get started."

Taking his lead, the band struck up a rowdy George Strait tune. Derrick mouthed the words automatically, his mind way ahead of this moment.

When their set was nearly finished, just before the band took a break, Derrick said, "I've got one more song before we take a break. I wrote this one for someone special who's here tonight, and I hope she likes it." He looked right at Kara.

She smiled as she looked back at him.

Derrick took a breath and began to sing.

"Some years ago I didn't know that she would be the one…."

As he sang, he watched Kara grow serious, tears filling her eyes. He held her gaze, revealing everything in his heart to her through the words of her song.

"…one thing that I know for sure,
Without you I am lost.
So I'll ask you just one question,
No matter what the cost…."

Her eyes widened, and he kept right on playing.
It felt as if they were the only two in the room.

"I'm hoping one day down the road,
you'll proudly take my name.
But until and if that day does come,
I'll wait for you right here…"

Derrick strummed the cords on his guitar, pur-
posely pausing…deliberately switching gears.

"And if you never come around
I'll sit here crying in my beer."

The crowd laughed as he finished with a fancy
guitar lick.

Then he laid down his Gibson and stepped to the
edge of the stage, microphone in hand. He looked
out at Kara.

"Kara, I'm trying to make you laugh, because
that's what I'd like to do a whole lot of with you in
the future." She didn't look away—a good sign.
"I've never been any good expressing my feelings,

except behind a guitar. I'm telling you this in front of our friends, family…our neighbors…because I don't want to hide my feelings any more."

He stepped down off the stage, and the spotlight followed him as he walked to her table. The crowd murmured.

"Everybody here knows what you've been through, Kara. And I know it's too soon to ask you the question I'd most like to ask. But—" He reached into his shirt pocket, and the crowd went wild, whistling, calling out encouragement. "It's not what y'all are thinking," Derrick said.

He pulled out the necklace he'd bought two days ago—a sterling silver heart on a chain. He dangled it from his free hand, still holding the microphone in the other. "I'm stepping out from behind my guitar to tell you that I love you—" the crowd whooped again "—and that I'll wait as long as it takes."

Kara had both hands over her mouth.

He held out the necklace. "I had this heart engraved, and I hope you'll wear it until I can replace it with a diamond ring…. When and if you'll have me."

The women in the bar went wild.

"You go, girl!"

"Woo-hoo! *Yeah*, baby!"

"I'll take it if she doesn't!"

Kara laughed, blinking rapidly. Then she stood and took the microphone from him.

"Oh, I'll wear it all right," she said to the crowd. Then she looked into his eyes. "And FYI, cowboy, I love you, too." She threw her arms around his neck and planted a kiss on his lips that had everyone in the honky-tonk hooting.

Derrick kissed her back as the roomful of people melted into the background.

His backup singer stepped up to the microphone. "Aw, hell. How do you top that?" Laughter. "I'd say this is the perfect moment for a country love song. Boys." He turned and spoke to the band, and they began to play.

All around, couples made their way to the dance floor. Some of them paid a hurried congratulations, or threw out a joking word or two as they passed by. But Derrick barely heard them. Barely heard the song, even.

He took Kara in his arms. "Dance with me?"

"Not until you put this on." She held out the heart necklace.

"Well, all right. But I think it'd look better on you." She laughed—the sound full of joy.

He brushed her hair out of the way, and fastened the chain around her neck, then placed a kiss against Kara's skin where the clasp rested. "Did you read the inscription?"

"I did." She kissed him again, her eyes saying more than her words.

As they danced, as he pressed his chest to hers, Derrick could practically feel the warmth of the words he'd had engraved on each side of the heart.

Derrick and Kara. Now and forever.

And an eternity beyond.

EPILOGUE

A year and a half later

THE DRIVEWAY TO THE RANCH was almost a mile long…perfect for a young man with a learner's permit to practice.

Connor grinned as he sat behind the wheel of the Ford he and Kara had once run into a baler. Only now, the truck was equipped with hand controls that enabled him to keep it between the lines.

"Can I drive to town this time?" he asked. "Please?"

From her place in the center of the bench seat, Kara laughed. "Ask your dad. I'm not going to be held responsible for that one."

She glanced at Derrick, riding shotgun with Lady crammed in between them. He looked as eager as Connor did.

"Well, seeing as how it's Christmastime," he said, "I suppose we can let you."

"We're only going to the tree lot," Connor said. "It's not like it's a hundred miles away."

"We're going to need a big tree," Kara said. "To put all those presents underneath."

She knew he'd love the shiny black Takamine guitar they'd gotten him, especially since he hardly bothered with the refurbished laptop he'd paid for himself, unless it was to do homework. Instead, Connor spent most of his time helping Melanie and Lisa at the riding center, and playing guitar and writing music with his dad.

The ranch itself had been made possible because of the success of Derrick's music. A new country star, recently discovered on a televised reality show, had made their dreams come true when he'd agreed to listen to Derrick's demo tape of "Heaven." He'd bought the song for more money than Kara had ever seen.

Six months ago, she'd sold the house she'd shared with Evan. Derrick had put his house on the market as well, and they'd finally gotten an offer on it two months ago.

Kara didn't need the predicted snow to have a white Christmas.

At the tree lot, they picked out a huge Scotch pine, and Connor razzed Derrick as the two of them attempted to load it into the Ford.

"Hey, Dad, I'm in a wheelchair, and I'm holding up my end better than you are. What's the matter, are you getting weak in your old age?"

His voice had deepened and matured, and he'd

grown and filled out as he approached his sixteenth birthday. He looked more like Derrick every day.

"Old, hell," Derrick retorted, "you've got the light end."

Standing there, Kara wished she could put the picture father and son made on a Christmas card, and save it forever.

She and Derrick still hadn't set a date for their wedding, but they weren't in a hurry. Kara took comfort in knowing that when she did walk down the aisle, Carolyn and Vernon Mertz would be there to wish them well. And Liz, too.

As though her thoughts had conjured her, Liz suddenly appeared, strolling along the sidewalk across the street. Kara opened her mouth to shout a greeting, then did a double take.

Liz wasn't alone.

Shawn Rutherford walked beside her. And he'd slipped his arm around her waist!

"Well, I'll be."

"What?" Derrick looked up. He grinned when he saw Liz and Shawn. "Guess it's a season of miracles all right."

"Yeah, and it'll be a miracle if we get this tree loaded before Christmas is over," Connor said. "You'd better help the old man, Kara."

They'd celebrated Derrick's thirty-third birthday just days ago.

"Hey, watch it," Derrick said. "Or I'll take back the saddle Santa brought you for your horse."

"Derrick!" Kara smacked his arm. "You weren't supposed to tell!"

"He already saw it. I couldn't exactly hide it under the bed."

"You're too much." Leaving father and son to their banter, Kara walked across the street.

Liz and Shawn were laughing as they window-shopped the row of old-fashioned stores in Sage Bend's main block.

"Happy holidays," Kara said.

Liz whirled around, her cheeks rosy from the cold. She blushed an even deeper shade of red, but her eyes sparkled.

"Kara!" She gave her a hug. "You know Shawn, don't you?"

"I do."

"Nice to see you, Kara."

"You, too." She smiled.

"I was just telling Shawn we need to get something really special for you and Derrick for Christmas."

Kara leaned in and kissed Liz on the cheek. "You already have," she whispered. "You look wonderful." They both knew she wasn't talking about Liz's new outfit.

"Thanks." Liz looked at Shawn with adoration. "Shawn and I bumped into each other at the Silver

Spur. He asked me to dance, and well..." She laughed.

Soft, fluffy flakes of snow began to drift down.

Across the street, Derrick called Kara's name.

"I'd better run. It was good seeing you, Shawn. And you, too, Liz." Kara hugged her, then lowered her voice. "Looks like Danita missed the boat."

"Oh, Kara." But Liz practically glowed.

"See you later." Kara turned and headed back, glad she hadn't missed her boat.

Glad she had a family to call her own.

But most of all, she thanked God for the man who made every day worth getting out of bed for—and then some.

It was definitely a white Christmas.

* * * * *

Set in darkness beyond the ordinary world.
Passionate tales of life and death.
With characters' lives ruled by laws the everyday
world can't begin to imagine.

Introducing NOCTURNE, a spine-tingling
new line from Silhouette Books.

The thrills and chills begin with
UNFORGIVEN by Lindsay McKenna

Plucked from the depths of hell, former military sharpshooter Reno Manchahi was hired by the government to kill a thief, but he had a mission of his own. Descended from a family of shape-shifters, Reno vowed to get the revenge he'd thirsted for all these years. But his mission went awry when his target turned out to be a powerful seductress, Magdalena Calen Hernandez, who risked everything to battle a potent evil. Suddenly, Reno had to transform himself into a true hero and fight the enemy that threatened them all. He had to become a Warrior for the Light....

Turn the page for a sneak preview of
UNFORGIVEN by Lindsay McKenna.
On sale September 26, wherever books are sold.

Chapter 1

One shot...one kill.

The sixteen-pound sledgehammer came down with such fierce power that the granite boulder shattered instantly. A spray of glittering mica exploded into the air and sparkled momentarily around the man who wielded the tool as if it were a weapon. Sweat ran in rivulets down Reno Manchahi's drawn, intense face. Naked from the waist up, the hot July sun beating down on his back, he hefted the sledgehammer skyward once more. Muscles in his thick forearms leaped and biceps bulged. Even his breath was focused on the boulder. In his mind's eye, he pictured Army General Robert Hampton's fleshy, arrogant fifty-year-old features on the rock's surface. Air exploded from between his lips as he brought the avenging hammer down. The boulder pulverized beneath his funneled hatred.

One shot...one kill...

Nostrils flaring, he inhaled the dank, humid heat and drew it deep into his massive lungs. Revenge allowed Reno to endure his imprisonment at a U.S. Navy brig near San Diego, California. Drops of sweat were flung in all directions as the crack of his sledgehammer claimed a third stone victim. Mouth taut, Reno moved to the next boulder.

The other prisoners in the stone yard gave him a wide berth. They always did. They instinctively felt his simmering hatred, the palpable revenge in his cinnamon-colored eyes, was more than skin-deep.

And they whispered he was different.

Reno enjoyed being a loner for good reason. He came from a medicine family of shape-shifters. But even this secret power had not protected him—or his family. His wife, Ilona, and his three-year-old daughter, Sarah, were dead. Murdered by Army General Hampton in their former home on USMC base in Camp Pendleton, California. Bitterness thrummed through Reno as he savagely pushed the toe of his scarred leather boot against several smaller pieces of gray granite that were in his way.

The sun beat down upon Manchahi's naked shoulders, grown dark red over time, shouting his half-Apache heritage. With his straight black hair grazing his thick shoulders, copper skin and broad face with high cheekbones, everyone knew he was Indian. When he'd first arrived at the brig, some of the prisoners taunted him and called him Geronimo. Something strange happened to Reno during his fight with the name-calling prisoners. Leaning down after he'd won the scuffle, he'd snarled into each of their bloodied faces that if they were going to call him anything, they would call him *gan*, which was the Apache word for *devil*.

His attackers had been shocked by the wounds on their faces, the deep claw marks. Reno recalled doubling his fist as they'd attacked him en masse. In that split second, he'd gone into an altered state of consciousness. In times of danger, he transformed into a jaguar. A deep, growling sound had emitted from his throat as he defended himself in the three-against-one fracas. It all happened so fast that he thought he had imagined it. He'd seen his hands morph into a forearm and paw, claws extended. The slashes left on the three men's faces after the fight told him he'd begun to shape-shift. A fist made bruises and swelling; not four perfect, deep claw marks. Stunned and anxious, he hid the knowledge of what else he was from these prisoners. Reno's only defense was to make all the prisoners so damned scared of him and remain a loner.

Alone. Yeah, he was alone, all right. The steel hammer swept downward with hellish ferocity. As the granite groaned in protest, Reno shut his eyes for just a moment. Sweat dripped off his nose and square chin.

Straightening, he wiped his furrowed, wet brow

and looked into the pale blue sky. What got his attention was the startling cry of a red-tailed hawk as it flew over the brig yard. Squinting, he watched the bird. Reno could make out the rust-colored tail on the hawk. As a kid growing up on the Apache reservation in Arizona, Reno knew that all animals that appeared before him were messengers.

Brother, what message do you bring me? Reno knew one had to ask in order to receive. Allowing the sledgehammer to drop to his side, he concentrated on the hawk who wheeled in tightening circles above him.

Freedom! the hawk cried in return.

Reno shook his head, his black hair moving against his broad, thickset shoulders. *Freedom? No way, Brother. No way.* Figuring that he was making up the hawk's shrill message, Reno turned away. Back to his rocks. Back to picturing Hampton's smug face.

Freedom!

* * * * *

Look for UNFORGIVEN by Lindsay McKenna,
the spine-tingling launch title from
Silhouette Nocturne ™.
Available September 26, wherever books are sold.

Introducing...

n o c t u r n e

a spine-tingling new line
from Silhouette Books.

These paranormal romances will
seduce you with dark, passionate tales
that stretch the boundaries of conflict,
desire, and life and death, weaving
a tapestry of sensual thrills and chills!

Don't miss the first book...

UNFORGIVEN

by *USA TODAY* bestselling author

LINDSAY McKENNA

Launching October 2006,
wherever books are sold.

Silhouette® BOMBSHELL™

On their twenty-first birthday,
the Crosse triplets discover
that each of them is destined
to carry their family's legacy
with the dark side.

DARKHEART & CROSSE

A new miniseries
from author

Harper ALLEN

Follow each triplet's story:

Dressed to Slay—October 2006
Unveiled family secrets lead sophisticated
Megan Crosse into the world of
shape-shifters and slayers.

Vampaholic—November 2006
Sexy Kat Crosse fears her dark future as a vampire
until a special encounter reveals her true fate.

Dead Is the New Black—January 2007
Tash Crosse will need to become the strongest
of them all to face a deadly enemy.

Available at your favorite retail outlet.

Silhouette Desire

**Introducing an exciting appearance
by legendary
New York Times bestselling author**

DIANA PALMER
HEARTBREAKER

He's the ultimate bachelor...
but he may have just met
the one woman to change his ways!

Join the drama in the story of a confirmed
bachelor, an amnesiac beauty and their
unexpected passionate romance.

---

*"Diana Palmer is a mesmerizing storyteller
who captures the essence of what
a romance should be."—Affaire de Coeur*

**Heartbreaker *is available from Silhouette Desire
in September 2006.***

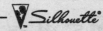

THE PART-TIME WIFE

by *USA TODAY* bestselling author

Maureen Child

Abby Talbot was the belle of Eastwick society;
the perfect hostess and wife. If only her
husband were more attentive. But when
she sets out to teach him a lesson and files
for divorce, Abby quickly learns her husband's
true identity...and exposes them to scandals
and drama galore!

On sale October 2006 from Silhouette Desire!

Available wherever books are sold,
including most bookstores, supermarkets,
discount stores and drug stores.